Call of the Cosmos

By

Charlotte Adams

Zara's Path to Exploration

As a child, Zara had always been fascinated by the stars. She would spend hours staring up at the night sky, imagining herself soaring among them. Her parents, both engineers, nurtured her love of science and encouraged her to pursue her dreams.

Zara grew up on the planet "Auroria," a place of beauty, wonder, and light, which further fueled and inspired Zara's love of science and exploration.

Auroria was a rich and vibrant environment, with a lush and diverse ecosystem. The planet had a breathable atmosphere, with an oxygen content similar to Earth's, allowing Zara to spend time outside without needing special equipment.

At night, the sky was a beautiful sight to behold, with a clear view of the stars and the Milky Way galaxy. Auroria's location in the galaxy provided a stunning view of nearby nebulae and star clusters, inspiring Zara's fascination with the stars and the universe beyond her world.

Overall, the planet was a welcoming and inspiring place for Zara to grow up, providing her with the environment and support she needed to pursue her dreams and become a starship captain.

By age six, Zara was already reading books meant for much older students. She had a natural talent for grasping complex concepts and solving difficult problems. Her parents decided to enroll her in advanced classes, where she quickly became a star pupil.

Zara's teachers were amazed by her intelligence and work ethic. She would often complete assignments and solve equations far beyond her peers' scope. Her classmates looked up to her and often asked her for help with their own work.

As Zara continued to excel academically, she became more and more focused on pursuing a career in science. She would spend her free time conducting experiments, building spacecraft models, and studying the latest discoveries in astronomy and physics. Her passion and dedication were unmatched, and it soon became apparent that she was destined for great things.

Despite her parents' initial concerns about their daughter being too young for advanced classes, they quickly realized that Zara was indeed a prodigy. Zara's childhood would unfold a symphony of intellectual curiosity as her parents orchestrated an environment that nurtured her burgeoning prodigious talents. Recognizing the spark of brilliance within their daughter, they embarked on a journey to cultivate her mind, crafting an educational landscape tailored to her exceptional abilities.

The family home transformed into a haven of learning. Zara's parents, both accomplished scientists in their own right, curated an extensive library that spanned the realms of physics, astronomy, and mathematics. Early evenings were spent engaged in spirited discussions, with Zara absorbing the intricate theories and concepts that danced through the air like cosmic constellations.

Her father introduced her to complex problem-solving techniques to enhance her mathematical prowess. He encouraged her to explore the world of abstract mathematics. Zara, with an insatiable thirst for knowledge, eagerly embraced these challenges, delving into equations that would leave seasoned scholars awestruck.

Her mother, an astrophysicist, took Zara on nocturnal explorations beneath the star-studded canopy. Armed with a telescope, they would venture into the backyard, unlocking the secrets of the cosmos. Zara's young eyes, wide with wonder, traced the paths of celestial bodies, and her mind soared through the infinite expanse of the universe.

The educational tapestry woven for Zara extended beyond conventional subjects. Art, music, and literature became integral threads, intertwining with the scientific foundation. Zara's parents believed in fostering a holistic intellect where creativity and analytical thinking coexisted harmoniously.

In addition to academic pursuits, Zara's parents exposed her to diverse experiences. They frequented museums, attended lectures by esteemed scholars, and engaged with the scientific community. Zara found herself amid luminaries, absorbing knowledge like a celestial sponge.

Her parents, initially concerned about the social ramifications of placing a young prodigy in advanced classes, soon realized that Zara's peers were as enchanted by her intellect as they were. Zara, though younger, became a source of inspiration, her passion infectious and her intellect a beacon that drew others into the orbit of discovery.

In this carefully crafted environment, Zara's prodigious talents flourished. Her parents, mentors, and guides navigated the delicate balance of nurturing a child prodigy, ensuring that every facet of her potential was explored and refined. The echoes of those formative years resonated throughout her life, shaping the trajectory of the prodigious explorer she would become.

Zara's childhood was marked by a tireless pursuit of knowledge and a deep love for science. Her early successes in the fields of astronomy, mathematics, and science set her on a path that would eventually lead her to become one of the most respected and accomplished explorers in the galaxy.

Zara's passion for science and astronomy was not limited to academic pursuits. As she learned more and more about the mysteries of the universe, she began to dream of one day exploring those wonders for herself, gazing up at the night sky and imagining what it would be like to travel among the stars.

As she grew older, Zara became increasingly focused on turning her dreams into reality. She would spend her free time studying the latest space technologies and following the careers of famous astronauts and explorers. Her ultimate goal was to use her advanced knowledge to become a space traveler and explorer herself.

Zara's dream was not just about personal ambition. She believed space exploration was critical for advancing human knowledge and understanding of the universe. She saw herself as a part of a larger mission to discover new worlds, study the mysteries of the cosmos, and push the boundaries of human knowledge.

Zara's drive, intelligence, and passion for science would eventually lead her to the highest echelons of the space exploration community. As she looked out into the infinite expanse of the universe, she knew that she was living her childhood dream and that there was still so much more to discover.

<u>Thalia</u>

Thalia was Zara's childhood friend, and their bond was as close as can be among young kids growing up on Auroria. Their friendship could be traced to an unusual and unforeseen celestial event. It was a warm Auroria evening, the twin moons rising harmoniously, casting an enchanting iridescence upon the landscape. On that particular night, the sky held a secret that would spark a lifelong friendship.

As curious as ever, Zara had been gazing at the stars from her family's backyard observatory. Her parents were renowned astronomers on Auroria, and their passion had passed down to their daughter. Zara had an innate talent for deciphering the mysteries of the night sky. At the tender age of eight, she was already a budding stargazer.

Meanwhile, Thalia had been watching the same celestial spectacle from her home, not too far away. Although she didn't share Zara's love for the stars, the unusual alignment of planets had captured her attention that night. It was a rare occurrence, and Thalia felt compelled to learn more about it.

Zara's excitement was palpable as she tracked the phenomenon through her telescope. Her tiny fingers adjusted the lens precisely, capturing the celestial event with an infectious zeal.

Unbeknownst to her, she had gained an audience, albeit a silent one.

Thalia had been watching Zara's observatory from a distance, drawn to the brilliant glow of the telescope's lens. She was struck by Zara's unwavering focus and the passion that radiated from her as she explained the event to her parents. Something about Zara's enthusiasm, the way she spoke of the stars, resonated with Thalia, igniting a curiosity she hadn't known before.

Unable to contain her curiosity any longer, Thalia approached the observatory. Hesitant but fascinated, she introduced herself to Zara. Though different in their interests, the two girls found a connection that transcended their differences.

As the night continued, Zara eagerly shared her knowledge of the cosmos with Thalia, who, in turn, asked thoughtful questions and listened with genuine interest. It was a meeting of minds and spirits, and the stars above seemed to approve.

Their cosmic connection was undeniable. Zara's passion for space and Thalia's eagerness to learn set the stage for a friendship that would carry them through childhood and adulthood. Little did they know that their shared fascination with the universe would be the foundation upon which their remarkable journey together and the conflicts that would come would be built.

Both girls were fascinated with space exploration, but Thalia's dreams would take a darker turn.

The days on Auroria were long, but they were filled with endless wonders for Zara and Thalia. From a young age, they had been inseparable, their friendship forged in the strange, otherworldly beauty of their home planet.

Zara and Thalia often found themselves in the heart of the Auroria forest, where luminescent trees cast a soft, ethereal glow. The forest was their sanctuary, a place of secrets and shared dreams. As the twin moons of Auroria illuminated the night sky, the two friends would sit beneath the iridescent foliage, their eyes fixed on the stars.

Zara's fascination with the cosmos was evident from the beginning. She would point out constellations and planets, her voice filled with wonder. "Imagine what it's like out there, Thalia," she'd say, her eyes gleaming with the promise of uncharted territory. "To explore the universe, to touch the stars. That's my dream."

Thalia, always eager to support her friend, would listen with rapt attention. She didn't share Zara's enthusiasm for space, but she saw the passion in her eyes and knew it was something special. "If anyone can do it, Zara, it's you," she'd reply with a supportive smile.

The Darkness Begins

As Zara and Thalia delved deeper into the mysteries of Auroria's ancient spacecraft, their childhood explorations evolved into a passion that would later define their destinies. The remnants of interstellar journeys continued to captivate them, providing a backdrop for the dreams that were slowly turning into a cosmic reality. Zara, fueled by boundless curiosity and astronomical knowledge, and Thalia, with her knack for deciphering languages, formed an inseparable duo in their quest for understanding.

Their excursions became increasingly daring, revealing alien hieroglyphics that adorned the walls of the spacecraft. Thalia's linguistic prowess allowed them to unlock the stories left behind by ancient travelers, tales that whispered of an ominous force lurking in the cosmic shadows. Zara, ever the stargazer, mapped out the constellations on the vessels' star charts, envisioning the intricate cosmic highways that connected the universe.

The turning point arrived with the discovery of a concealed underground chamber within one of the spacecrafts. Illuminated by the soft glow of ancient technology, Zara and Thalia uncovered an intricately detailed star map. It was a celestial tapestry documenting the paths of explorers long gone — a testament to the boundless potential beyond Auroria. Zara's eyes sparkled with excitement as she traced the constellations with her fingers. "This could be our path, Thalia," she exclaimed. "We could follow the stars and make our own history."

Thalia's smile, once a mixture of admiration and concern, now carried an unsettling shadow. Her fascination with the ancient stories began to transform into a subtle influence, drawing her towards a darker path. "If anyone can do it," Thalia replied, her words laced with a mysterious undertone, "it's you, Zara."

Unbeknownst to them, these early adventures were sowing the seeds of a future marked by conflict as Thalia, under the subtle sway of malevolent forces, began to tread a path veiled in shadows. Influenced by these insidious currents, Thalia gradually succumbed to a path that led her into the heart of shadows. The celestial dreams she once shared with Zara, now distorted by ominous undertones, painted a foreboding picture of intertwined destinies yet irrevocably altered.

The malevolent forces that whispered to Thalia weren't mere figments of imagination; they were cosmic entities, ancient and hungry for the untapped power that lay within forbidden knowledge. These forces wrapped themselves around Thalia's intellect, their subtle but insistent influence guiding her toward secrets that transcended the boundaries of morality and sanity.

Thalia's perceptions shifted as she delved deeper into the forbidden realms, and the stars, once beacons of wonder, took on a more sinister glow. Their light, tainted by the malevolence that entwined her fate, cast eerie shadows on the cosmic canvases of her dreams. The celestial bodies became witnesses to her descent, their distant gleam reflecting the twisted journey she undertook under the darkening skies.

Thalia's mind, once a sanctuary of curiosity, now resonated with whispers from the malevolent forces. The forbidden symbols and algorithms she explored weren't merely intellectual pursuits but gateways to eldritch dimensions, realms where the malevolent forces lurked, hungering for souls willing to unravel the cosmic mysteries.

The dark forces sought to reshape Thalia's understanding of the universe and the fabric of reality itself. The shadows, once benign companions in the dance of starlight, now clung to her like sentient tendrils, guiding her steps through the labyrinthine corridors of forbidden knowledge.

Zara and Thalia's destinies diverged in the cosmic interplay of light and darkness. The forces that ensnared Thalia sought to exploit the cosmic balance, tipping it toward chaos and unveiling ancient powers that lay dormant in the cosmic tapestry. The stars, witnesses to the unfolding drama, twinkled with a knowing yet indifferent gleam, casting their ominous light on a friendship strained by the cosmic forces that played puppeteers to the fate of the two friends.

A Growing Divide

As the years passed, their trajectories veered in opposite directions. Driven by an unyielding determination, Zara delved into astrophysics, charting her course among the stars. Influenced by a burgeoning darkness, Thalia embraced her linguistic talents to unravel the secrets of a malevolent past.

The stars, witnesses to the growing divide between them, silently foreshadowed the challenges and conflicts that awaited. Little did Zara anticipate that the cosmic tapestry binding her and Thalia together would unravel into a narrative of cosmic proportions, with their destinies entangled in a battle between light and shadow.

Once an integral part of Zara's orbit during those formative years, Thalia experienced the same nurturing environment that kindled Zara's brilliance. However, the cosmic symphony that played in Zara's life had a different resonance for Thalia. While Zara's trajectory soared toward exploration and enlightenment, Thalia was drawn to the shadows, enticed by unseen forces.

In the shared haven of learning that Zara and Thalia inhabited, Thalia's mind absorbed the profound theories and cosmic wonders. Yet, an insatiable hunger for something beyond the realms of conventional knowledge gnawed at Thalia's intellect. The tapestry woven for her was threaded with darker hues, mysterious and alluring.

Much like Zara's, Thalia's parents were accomplished scientists, but their pursuits led them into the clandestine corridors of forbidden science. Thalia was exposed to the wonders of the universe and the enigmatic and often perilous realms that lay hidden in the cosmic shadows. While rooted in the sciences, her education delved into forbidden territories that whispered promises of power and secrets that could reshape reality.

As Zara embraced the equations of abstract mathematics, Thalia delved into arcane symbols and forbidden algorithms. Her nocturnal explorations beneath the star-studded canopy weren't guided solely by the pursuit of knowledge but also by a darker curiosity that sought the forbidden knowledge hidden within the cosmic expanse.

While Zara's parents sought to balance intellect with creativity, Thalia's upbringing blurred the lines between exploration and exploitation. The integration of art, music, and literature in Thalia's education was not a harmonious blend but a discordant symphony that echoed her soul's dissonance.

Unlike Zara, who became a source of inspiration for her peers, Thalia's intellect became a source of fear and fascination. The shadows cast by her unconventional pursuits became a veil that cloaked her in an enigmatic aura. Enchanted yet wary, her peers felt a magnetic pull toward her, drawn to the darkness that clung to Thalia like a cosmic shroud.

As the echoes of those formative years reverberated through Zara's life, shaping her into an explorer of the cosmos, they also left Thalia on a divergent path—a path that led her into the embrace of shadows, secrets, and the darker forces that lurked within the cosmic unknown. The cosmic symphony played different melodies for Zara and Thalia, setting the stage for a reunion fraught with uncharted complexities and hidden destinies.

Auroria, a planet bathed in the glow of its binary stars, held secrets in its celestial tapestry that extended beyond the eyes of its inhabitants. On this night, the air was crisp, carrying the scent of exotic flowers that bloomed under the light of the twin moons. The sky shimmered in a palette of hues as the stars cast their enchanting glow upon the landscape.

Zara and Thalia, anticipating the celestial spectacle that awaited them, embarked on their customary stargazing expedition during the annual event known as the "Luminary Cascade." This meteor shower, a breathtaking display of cosmic brilliance, was a cherished tradition on their planet, marked by the convergence of interstellar debris in the Aurorian atmosphere.

The air on Auroria was infused with a cool, refreshing breeze; the luminescent grass, a unique feature of the planet, served as their celestial viewing perch, creating an ethereal bed for the friends to recline upon. It emitted a soft, iridescent glow, responding to the energy of the meteor shower above.

As Zara and Thalia settled into their luminescent haven, the creatures of Auroria serenaded them with a melodic hum, adding a harmonious layer to the natural symphony. The binary stars, Auroria's celestial sentinels, cast their unwavering glow upon the landscape, creating an enchanting ambiance for the impending cosmic display.

The Luminary Cascade unfolded with a magnificent grandeur as if the heavens themselves had opened to reveal the inner workings of the cosmos. A myriad of meteors streaked across the sky, leaving ephemeral trails of incandescent light in their wake. Each meteor, a messenger from the far reaches of the universe, contributed to the celestial dance that unfolded above.

The meteor shower was not merely a random occurrence; it was an annual celestial ballet, a cosmic choreography that captivated the hearts and minds of Auroria's inhabitants. During the peak of the Luminary Cascade, meteors cascaded through the atmosphere at a rate of several hundred per hour, creating a mesmerizing display that rivaled the most intricate constellations.

Zara and Thalia, nestled among the luminescent grass, were awe-struck by the radiant beauty above. The meteors, varying in size and brightness, painted the night sky with trails of incandescent hues, creating a celestial tapestry that seemed to transcend time and space.

As the girls observed the cascade, the event became almost mythical. It was a reminder of the cosmic wonders that lay beyond their planet and fueled Zara's insatiable curiosity for the unknown. Little did they know that on this night, beneath the celestial shower, Thalia would deliver a prophecy that would cast a shadow over the very passion that had bound them together.

The Luminary Cascade, once a symbol of beauty and cosmic interconnectedness, now carried an undertone of foreboding, setting the stage for a journey that would unfold against the backdrop of the stars.

As the Luminary Cascade reached its zenith, Thalia's typically vivid eyes reflecting the mesmerizing display above underwent a transformation that caught Zara's attention. The luminescent glow from the meteor shower seemed to cast an ethereal radiance upon Thalia's features, accentuating the contours of her face.

A hush settled over the luminescent grass as Thalia's gaze fixed on the cosmic ballet. Her eyes, once warm and familiar, became pools of reflected starlight. They widened, taking on a depth that transcended the ordinary as if the universe itself had cast its reflection within them.

Thalia's features, now bathed in the ephemeral glow of the meteor shower, took on an otherworldly aura. The subtle luminescence of her skin seemed to harmonize with the celestial display, creating an illusion that she was an integral part of the cosmic dance unfolding above. Strands of her hair, kissed by the stars' glow, framed her face like strands of stardust.

As the celestial energy intensified, Thalia's physical presence seemed to dissolve into the night, and a serene stillness enveloped her. Her breathing became rhythmic, synchronized with the cosmic heartbeat echoing through the atmosphere. It was as if the very essence of the universe coursed through her veins, and she became a conduit for the cosmic forces at play.

Zara watched in awe as her friend, bathed in the astral glow, fell into a trance that transcended the boundaries of the material world. Thalia's connection to celestial energy became palpable, an invisible thread linking her to the tapestry above. The luminescent grass beneath her seemed to respond to her presence, emitting a gentle glow that mirrored the radiance of the meteor shower.

Thalia's voice, when it finally emerged, carried an ethereal quality in that moment of cosmic communion. Her words were not merely spoken; they resonated with a resonance that seemed to echo through the very fabric of space and time. She spoke of a future wrought with the interplay of destiny and the celestial energies that bound the universe together.

To Zara, Thalia appeared as a celestial oracle, a conduit for the cosmic revelations she was about to unveil. The luminescent glow, the reflection of the meteor shower in her eyes, and the ethereal quality of her voice painted a portrait of a friend momentarily transcending the confines of the mortal realm.

As Thalia began to share her vision, the grass beneath them seemed to shudder in acknowledgment. The meteor shower, once a symbol of beauty and wonder, now took on a weight of cosmic significance that would shape the destinies of Zara and Thalia in ways neither of them could have fathomed. The trance Thalia experienced during the Luminary Cascade became the catalyst for a prophecy that would linger in the air like a whispering echo of the stars, leaving Zara to grapple with the cosmic doubts that had taken root in her once-unshakable passion for exploration.

The Prophecy

Thalia's eyes, still reflecting the cosmic glow above, became windows into a vision that transcended the bounds of their tranquil stargazing haven. With each word, Thalia wove a tapestry of cosmic inevitability, and the air itself seemed to resonate with the echoes of her prophecy.

"In the celestial dance, Zara," Thalia began, her voice carrying the weight of cosmic revelation, "I witnessed the threads of your destiny entwined with the very fabric of the universe. A future unfolded, where your relentless pursuit of the stars unraveled the cosmic order, casting ripples of chaos across the galaxy."

Thalia's gestures mirrored the cosmic ballet they had witnessed, as if she were channeling the celestial energies surrounding them. Her words painted a vivid tableau of a galaxy plunged into turmoil; stars extinguished like distant whispers silenced by the cosmic winds.

"I saw constellations, once steadfast in the cosmic tapestry, distorted by the gravitational pull of your aspirations," Thalia continued, her eyes fixed on an unseen horizon. "The Luminary Cascade, once a celebration of our shared wonder, became the harbinger of cosmic discord. Stars blinked out, one by one, as the echoes of your pursuit reverberated through the cosmos."

Usually grounded in the tangible, Zara felt an ethereal chill as Thalia's vision unfolded. The luminescent grass beneath them shimmered in response to the celestial revelations as if acknowledging the cosmic weight of the prophecy.

"The binary stars, once our celestial guides, cast shadows over worlds unseen. Planets trembled, their orbits disrupted by the cosmic echoes of your insatiable curiosity," Thalia whispered, the weight of her words lingering in the air like a cosmic elegy.

A galaxy, once harmonious in its celestial dance, became a canvas painted with strokes of destruction. Once a beacon of inspiration, Zara's passion for space exploration now cast a long shadow over the cosmic tableau Thalia had witnessed.

"The luminescent grass, once aglow with the wonders of the cosmos, withered beneath the cosmic discord," Thalia concluded, her voice returning to the mortal realm. "Zara, in pursuing the unknown, you may unravel the very fabric that binds the stars. The Luminary Cascade, once a celebration of cosmic interconnectedness, may become the catalyst for an unforeseen cataclysm."

As Thalia's vision faded, the Luminary Cascade continued its celestial dance, but the once-spectacular meteor shower now carried an ominous undertone. Zara stood, caught between the awe of the meteor shower and the weight of Thalia's prophecy, feeling the cosmic threads of her destiny unraveling in the vast tapestry of the universe. The Luminary Cascade, a symbol of celestial beauty, now echoed with the haunting whispers of a prophecy that would linger in the air long after the meteor shower had subsided, leaving Zara to grapple with the cosmic doubts that had taken root in the fertile soil of her passion.

Doubt crept into Zara's heart like an insidious shadow. Thalia's vision was vivid, a haunting tableau of galactic upheaval, and the weight of its implications settled heavily on Zara's shoulders. The doubt that gnawed at her was born from her love for the cosmos, the very passion that had defined her existence. What if her dreams, her fervent desire to explore the universe, were the catalyst for an unforeseen cataclysm? Zara's mind became a battleground between her unwavering love for the stars and the unsettling prophecy that Thalia had woven into the fabric of their shared reality.

The seeds of doubt planted by Thalia's prophecy grew roots in Zara's soul, casting shadows over her once-clear vision of a cosmic odyssey. The meteor shower that had illuminated the Aurorian sky now left Zara grappling with an existential quandary, torn between her passion for exploration and the foreboding prophecy that threatened to eclipse her celestial dreams.

Shadows of Doubt

In the wake of Thalia's haunting prophecy, Zara found herself navigating uncharted territories within her own psyche. The once-unshakable foundation of her passion for space exploration now trembled under the weight of doubt. Once a celebration of cosmic wonders, the Luminary Cascade seemed to cast shadows that lingered over her every thought.

As she stood beneath the twin moons of Auroria, Zara grappled with the existential quandary that had taken root within her soul. Thalia's words echoed in the recesses of her mind, whispering doubts that reverberated like cosmic ripples.

Zara's response to the looming uncertainty was not to retreat from her dreams but to confront the shadows head-on. With a resolute determination that burned brighter than the binary stars above, she sought to reclaim the clarity of her vision.

In the following years, Zara immersed herself in the cosmic knowledge that had once been a source of boundless inspiration. She delved into the ancient texts left by explorers of old, sought the wisdom of Aurorian astronomers, and spent countless nights beneath the stars, seeking solace in the familiar embrace of the cosmos.

Each meteor streaking across the Aurorian sky was a testament to Zara's unwavering spirit. She studied the Luminary Cascade with a newfound intensity, hoping to discern a cosmic truth that would dispel the shadows of doubt. The celestial dance above, once a source of wonder, now became a canvas upon which she painted her determination.

As Zara approached her 18th birthday, the age at which she could apply for the United Interstellar Alliance (UIA), her resolve crystallized into a cosmic force of its own. Thalia's prophecy, though haunting, fueled Zara's determination to prove that her passion for exploration could coexist with the harmony of the universe.

Once ominous in their symbolic shadows, the binary stars became guiding lights for Zara's journey. She sought mentors among the seasoned spacefarers of Auroria, absorbing their wisdom and channeling their experiences into a reservoir of cosmic knowledge. The grass beneath her feet no longer whispered of doubts but cradled her with a gentle luminescence, a supportive foundation for the dreams that refused to be eclipsed.

With a heart aflame with cosmic curiosity and a mind resilient against the shadows, Zara prepared her application for the UIA. She harnessed the doubts planted by Thalia's prophecy and transformed them into a driving force that fueled her passion for exploration.

Zara's application, a testament to her unwavering commitment, carried the weight of celestial dreams and the resilience of a spirit unyielding in the face of doubt. As she embarked on this cosmic odyssey, the Luminary Cascade above, now devoid of shadows, became a cosmic witness to Zara's perseverance. This meteor shower illuminated the path of a determined explorer ready to defy the foreboding whispers of fate.

The United Interstellar Alliance

Zara was determined to make her dream of space travel a reality. She studied hard, excelling in mathematics, physics, and engineering. When she turned 18, she applied to the United Interstellar Alliance (UIA).

The United Interstellar Alliance (UIA) is the governing body of space exploration, established to promote collaboration and cooperation among the different civilizations and species in the galaxy.

The UIA comprises representatives from various member planets, each working together to advance scientific understanding, promote peaceful relations, and protect against threats to galactic security.

The UIA comprises both elected and appointed officials, focusing on maintaining transparency, accountability, and democratic principles in its decision-making processes. The UIA is also supported by various specialized departments and agencies, including scientific research institutes, diplomatic corps, and military defense forces.

The importance of the UIA lies in its ability to bring together different cultures and civilizations to work towards common goals. By promoting cooperation and collaboration, the UIA has advanced scientific knowledge and promoted peaceful relations among its member planets. The UIA also serves as a platform for sharing resources and expertise, providing support and assistance to member planets when needed.

In addition, the UIA is responsible for maintaining galactic security and protecting against threats from hostile entities such as pirates, rogue factions, or aggressive empires. By pooling the resources and capabilities of its member planets, the UIA can respond to such threats promptly and effectively, preserving peace and stability throughout the galaxy.

However, the UIA does have enemies, and the Terran Empire is one of them. The Terran Empire is a powerful and aggressive military empire that seeks to dominate and control other civilizations in the galaxy. The Empire sees the UIA as a threat to its expansionist goals and has previously engaged in numerous conflicts and hostilities with the UIA.

The Terran Empire's aggression has put it at odds with the UIA's goals of promoting peace and cooperation among different civilizations in the galaxy. As a result, the UIA has been forced to take a defensive stance against the Terran Empire, engaging in various military campaigns and diplomatic efforts to contain the Empire's influence and protect its member planets.

Rumors circulated like cosmic whispers about the origins of the Terran Empire, an enigmatic force that seemed to materialize from the cosmic abyss itself. The galaxy found itself under the looming shadow of an empire whose formation remained shrouded in mystery. No one could ascertain who pulled the strings of its vast machinery, and the question of leadership became an elusive puzzle for even the most astute astronomers and historians. It was as if the Terran Empire emerged from the cosmic void, driven by an insatiable hunger for dominance and control. The galactic community, wary of the Empire's power and aggression, struggled to fathom the true architects behind its rise.

With its mysterious origins and aggressive expansionism, the Terran Empire loomed as a formidable adversary in the cosmic ballet, and its clash with the UIA would unleash forces that transcended the boundaries of space and time.

While the UIA seeks to resolve conflicts peacefully and diplomatically whenever possible, it recognizes the need to defend itself and its member planets against hostile forces like the Terran Empire. As such, the UIA maintains a robust military presence and advanced defensive capabilities to deter potential threats and respond to any aggression directed toward its member planets.

Zara's interest in joining the UIA was motivated by curiosity, exploration, and the desire to contribute to advancing scientific knowledge and interstellar cooperation. The UIA is a prominent organization in the galaxy, with a significant role in exploring and understanding the universe beyond individual planets. As a lover of science, Zara was drawn to the UIA as an opportunity to pursue her passions and positively impact the galaxy as a whole.

The thought of battle with the enemies of the UIA was the furthest thing on Zara's life plan.

The UIA's cadet program is a rigorous training program designed to prepare aspiring starship captains and crew members for space exploration and defense challenges. The process for being accepted into the cadet program typically involves several rounds of testing and evaluation, including aptitude tests, physical fitness assessments, and psychological evaluations.

After anxious weeks of waiting, the momentous message from the United Interstellar Alliance (UIA) arrived, heralding Zara's acceptance into their prestigious exploration program like a cosmic proclamation. The news sparked a radiant glow within her, and Zara was overwhelmed with exhilaration and gratitude. The joy that bubbled within her was infectious, a testament to the crystallization of her dreams as they transformed into the tangible reality of a cosmic odyssey awaiting her.

In the quiet solitude of her room, Zara absorbed the weight of the message, her heart racing with the anticipation of the adventures that awaited in the cosmic unknown. As she envisioned the vast expanse of uncharted territories, she couldn't help but revel in the cosmic symphony that echoed the promise of discovery and exploration.

Unbeknownst to Zara, Thalia, once her closest confidante, observed the news from the shadows with a facade of feigned excitement. However, a tumultuous storm of conflicting emotions raged within the recesses of Thalia's being. The announcement triggered a bittersweet struggle within her. On the one hand, she couldn't deny the genuine excitement for her childhood friend's achievements and the cosmic journey Zara was about to embark on. On the other hand, Thalia grappled with the shadows of her cosmic visions, harboring a foreboding sense of destiny that drove her to subtly undermine Zara's cosmic ambitions.

As Zara danced on the precipice of a cosmic voyage, Thalia's reactions masked a cosmic vendetta that would cast shadows over their intertwined destinies. The struggle within Thalia mirrored the cosmic conflict playing out in her soul — a battle between the genuine affection for her friend and the insidious influence of the malevolent forces that sought to manipulate destinies for their own dark purposes. Little did Zara know that her cosmic ambitions were entwined with the unseen threads of a cosmic vendetta, setting the stage for a complex interplay of light and darkness in the chapters that lay ahead.

Cosmic Crucible

Having earned her place in the United Interstellar Alliance (UIA), Zara entered a rigorous training program designed to mold her into an adept explorer capable of navigating the vast expanse of the cosmos. The UIA, recognizing the inherent challenges and dangers of space exploration, curated a comprehensive curriculum that blended intellectual acumen with physical prowess, ensuring their recruits were prepared for the myriad challenges that awaited them.

Zara's days at the UIA began with intensive theoretical courses, delving into astrophysics, celestial navigation, and interstellar communications. Seasoned astronomers and explorers, renowned in the cosmic community, served as instructors, imparting their wisdom and expertise to the eager recruits. Zara absorbed knowledge like a cosmic sponge, learning to decipher the celestial tapestry and gaining insights into the mysteries of the universe.

Practical training sessions followed, where Zara honed her spacecraft operation and maintenance skills. She navigated simulations of challenging cosmic environments, learning to handle the complexities of space travel, gravitational anomalies, and unforeseen cosmic phenomena. The UIA's state-of-the-art spacecraft simulators provided a realistic experience, immersing Zara in the unpredictable nature of space.

Physical training played a crucial role in the UIA's curriculum, recognizing that the demands of space exploration extended beyond intellectual capacities. Zara underwent rigorous fitness regimens, including strength and endurance exercises designed to prepare her for the physical strains of extended space missions. The UIA emphasized the importance of peak physical conditions for astronauts, as the microgravity environment of space required a robust cardiovascular system and muscular strength to counteract the effects of prolonged weightlessness.

Team-building exercises were integral to the UIA training, fostering camaraderie and cooperation among the recruits. Zara worked alongside diverse individuals, each bringing their unique skills and backgrounds to the cosmic table. The UIA emphasized the collaborative nature of space exploration, instilling in its recruits the ability to function seamlessly as a team, especially in the face of unforeseen challenges.

Survival training sessions took Zara to the outer edges of her comfort zone. UIA instructors simulated scenarios that mirrored potential challenges in uncharted territories, teaching recruits essential survival skills in hostile environments. Zara learned to adapt to the unpredictable nature of space, mastering the art of resource management and crisis response.

The multifaceted training at the UIA aimed to create well-rounded explorers capable of navigating the cosmos with a combination of intellectual prowess, physical fitness, and resilience in the face of adversity. The UIA recognized that the vast unknown required more than just technical know-how; it demanded a holistic approach to exploration, ensuring that every recruit was not only a master of their craft but also a beacon of adaptability and innovation in the cosmic crucible that awaited them beyond the stars.

During the cadet program, cadets are evaluated and tested on their progress to identify those with the skills and temperament to become effective UIA officers. Upon graduation from the program, successful cadets are typically assigned to a UIA vessel, where they will continue their training and gain practical experience under the guidance of experienced officers.

Despite the rigorous programs, Zara excelled. She threw herself into her studies, devouring every piece of information she could find on space travel, alien species, and intergalactic politics.

As Zara ascended through the United Interstellar Alliance (UIA) ranks, her innate leadership qualities shone brighter with each passing cosmic challenge. Recognizing her exceptional capabilities, Zara was swiftly promoted to the esteemed position of squad leader during her inaugural year of training. Her fellow cadets admired her intellectual prowess, unyielding determination, and unswerving commitment to the UIA's overarching mission of exploration and interstellar diplomacy. The corridors of the UIA's training facility buzzed with tales of Zara's leadership finesse and her uncanny ability to inspire camaraderie among the diverse group of future explorers.

Little did Zara know that unbeknownst to her, Thalia, driven by her own shadows and cosmic visions, had begun a clandestine campaign to undermine the very foundations of Zara's celestial dreams, setting in motion a cosmic struggle that would reverberate through the cosmos. Her once-shared dreams of exploration now twisted into a cosmic nightmare, Thalia sought to cast a veil of darkness over Zara's celestial aspirations.

Ever the adept infiltrator, Thalia found subtle ways to tamper with Zara's equipment without leaving a trace. Under the guise of friendship, she would ostensibly visit Zara's quarters in the UIA training facility to share tales of galactic wonders. In these moments, Thalia, cloaked in the shadows of deception, would discreetly damage the delicate instruments that Zara relied on for her cosmic studies.

The telescopic lenses, the tools that once united them in exploring the unknown, fell victim to Thalia's clandestine tampering efforts. By making minute adjustments, imperceptible to the untrained eye, Thalia threw off the precision of Zara's observations, leading her to question the reliability of the instruments she held dear.

Simultaneously, Thalia orchestrated a campaign of misinformation, feeding Zara false narratives about the dangers lurking in the cosmic expanse. She exploited Zara's lingering doubts, painting a portrait of the universe as a hostile and unforgiving abyss, ready to devour the unprepared explorer. With a disarming smile that concealed her ulterior motives, Thalia spun tales of cosmic anomalies, malevolent entities, and interstellar perils that existed solely in the shadowy recesses of her imagination.

Thalia's deceptive web extended to Zara's research notes, once a testament to their shared passion for exploration. Pages disappeared, vital calculations were altered, and the cosmic coordinates Zara meticulously recorded were subtly manipulated. The fabric of Zara's cosmic knowledge began to unravel as if the very essence of the universe conspired to distort her understanding of the cosmos.

Unsuspecting of the shadows that encroached upon her cosmic journey, Zara felt the weight of

Thalia's subtle manipulations. Once a symbol of cosmic interconnectedness, the Luminary Cascade now cast an eerie glow over Zara's struggles. Thalia's machinations, born from a vision that transcended reason, played out in the clandestine dance of shadows that eclipsed Zara's once-clear vision.

As Zara delved deeper into her UIA training, the challenges mounted, and the shadows of Thalia's manipulations deepened. Zara grappled with the sabotaged equipment, the distorted information, and the ever-present doubts clawed at the edges of her celestial dreams. Unbeknownst to her, Thalia's cosmic vendetta against the UIA, born from a vision of destruction, had cast a long shadow over the cosmic odyssey that awaited Zara, setting the stage for a confrontation that would transcend the boundaries of friendship and plunge them into a galactic conflict fueled by shadows and cosmic betrayals.

Stellar Ascension: Zara's Odyssey through the UIA Ranks

As the years went by, Zara continued to rise through the ranks. Zara's journey through the ranks of the UIA was marked by hard work, dedication, and a solid commitment to excellence. She started as a young cadet, dreaming of commanding her own starship and exploring the vast reaches of space. Over time, she proved herself a capable and skilled officer, earning promotions and recognition from her superiors.

Zara's stellar journey into leadership commenced with her promotion to the esteemed rank of Ensign, a role that thrust her into the intricate web of responsibilities aboard a UIA vessel. As a junior officer, Zara immersed herself in a dynamic environment where each decision had cosmic consequences. The defining moment that solidified her reputation unfolded during an unexpected encounter with a celestial phenomenon that tested the mettle of the entire crew.

While on a routine exploration mission, their vessel became ensnared in the gravitational pull of a massive, unpredictable space anomaly. The ship's systems faltered, and panic rippled through the crew as alarms blared in the confined spaces of the UIA vessel. Zara's training kicked in amid the chaos, and she seamlessly assumed command of the situation.

Displaying an unparalleled command of navigation and piloting, Zara orchestrated a series of precise maneuvers to disentangle the ship from the anomaly's grasp. Her hands danced across the control panel with unwavering confidence, calibrating the ship's systems and compensating for the gravitational fluctuations threatening to destabilize their trajectory. The vessel held its breath as Zara's quick thinking and innate ability to work under pressure shone through.

In the aftermath of the crisis, the crew emerged unscathed, the ship intact and the mission salvaged. Zara's exceptional performance did not go unnoticed. Her superiors commended her for the precise execution of critical maneuvers, meticulous attention to detail, and leadership during intense cosmic adversity.

Zara's heroic feat during this mission became a cornerstone in her ascent through the ranks. The reputation she earned for her quick thinking and ability to maintain composure under pressure laid the groundwork for a stellar career that would see her rise to even greater heights within the UIA. This pivotal moment not only defined her early years as an officer but also set the stage for the cosmic challenges that lay ahead in her journey of exploration and leadership.

Zara's meteoric rise through the UIA ranks culminated in her promotion to the esteemed rank of Lieutenant. This position thrust her into a pivotal role at the heart of the ship's day-to-day operations. In this elevated position, Zara became the linchpin of the vessel's functionality, overseeing various responsibilities with unparalleled skill and dedication. Her multifaceted role involved managing the crew's training, equipment, and morale and delving into the realm of strategic innovation.

Driven by her insatiable curiosity and a commitment to advancing the frontiers of cosmic knowledge, Zara played a pivotal role in crafting groundbreaking strategies and tactics for exploration and scientific research. Drawing upon her diverse expertise in fields ranging from astrophysics to engineering, she spearheaded initiatives that pushed the boundaries of the UIA's capabilities.

During one particularly challenging mission, Zara encountered a previously uncharted celestial phenomenon that posed unique challenges. Undeterred, she led her team in brainstorming sessions, fostering an environment where creativity and expertise coalesced. Zara's strategic acumen shone through as she devised innovative approaches to navigate the unexplored cosmic anomaly, ensuring both the crew's safety and the mission's success.

Her leadership in developing new strategies didn't stop at the ship's helm. Zara actively engaged with fellow officers and scientists, fostering collaboration that transcended disciplinary boundaries. This collaborative spirit led to the creation of pioneering exploration methodologies and cutting-edge scientific protocols. Zara's commitment to pushing the envelope of exploration became a driving force behind the UIA's reputation for innovation in the cosmic community.

As Lieutenant, Zara's legacy extended beyond the immediate demands of ship operations. Her strategic prowess and innovative thinking not only elevated the UIA's efficiency in navigating the cosmic unknown but also solidified her status as a trailblazer in the field of interstellar exploration. The celestial tapestry, once veiled in mystery, unfurled new chapters under Zara's leadership, each page a testament to her commitment to advancing the frontiers of cosmic knowledge and forging a path toward a future where the universe's secrets could be unraveled by those bold enough to explore its depths.

As Zara continued to rise through the ranks, she was promoted to the rank of Commander, where she assumed even greater responsibility for the success of the missions she was tasked with. She was responsible for the safety and well-being of her crew, as well as the mission's overall success. She developed strong leadership skills, such as delegation, communication, and decision-making, which allowed her to inspire her team to achieve their best.

Finally, after years of dedicated service and outstanding performance, Zara was promoted to Captain, the highest rank in the UIA. In this role, she had the honor of commanding her own starship, leading her crew on various missions, including exploratory, scientific, diplomatic, and military missions. She was known for her boldness, creativity, and unwavering commitment to her mission's success.

Through her years of service and promotion, Zara developed a strong sense of leadership, integrity, and responsibility. She learned to trust her instincts, to work collaboratively with others, and to make difficult decisions under pressure. These experiences shaped her into a leader respected and admired by her colleagues and superiors alike and well-prepared to lead her team on their mission to explore the distant planet of Eurydice, fulfilling a lifelong dream.

As Zara's ascent unfolded, Thalia, once a childhood friend, observed the transformation with conflicting emotions. Zara's journey, marked by developing a robust leadership ethos, unwavering integrity, and a keen sense of responsibility, resonated deeply with Thalia.

Despite their shared history, Thalia couldn't ignore the growing divide between them as Zara honed her ability to trust instincts, collaborate effectively, and make decisive choices under pressure. The respect and admiration Zara earned from colleagues and superiors became a source of envy for Thalia, fostering a sense of resentment. Zara's pursuit of a lifelong dream, leading a team to explore the distant planet of Eurydice, fueled Thalia's conflicting emotions—anticipation for the monumental mission and burgeoning darkness that hinted at a turbulent path ahead. The once-shared pride now mingled with a sense of foreboding as Thalia grappled with the realization that Zara's journey had shaped her into a formidable leader and set the stage for an ominous confrontation between childhood friends and adversaries.

Shadows of Betrayal

In the quiet corridors of the mission headquarters, whispers of doubt and mistrust slithered through the air like venomous serpents. Consumed by her dark vision, Thalia orchestrated a campaign to undermine Zara's credibility. The rumors, carefully crafted by Thalia's insidious machinations, spoke of Zara as a clandestine threat, a shadow lurking within the heart of the mission to Eurydice.

The whispers hinted at Zara's alleged allegiance to an unknown faction, painting her as a double agent plotting to sabotage the very expedition she passionately led. They questioned her loyalty to the mission, casting doubt on the authenticity of her dreams and aspirations. Friends who once stood beside Zara with unwavering support now exchanged wary glances, unsure whether the woman they believed in was indeed who she seemed to be.

Zara engrossed in the final preparations for the journey, remained oblivious to the venomous rumors encircling her. The sense of foreboding that hung in the air intensified with each passing day. Even family members, swayed by the carefully constructed whispers, began to regard Zara with uncertain eyes, their expressions mirroring the darkness that crept into the fabric of their once unbreakable bonds.

As the rumors reached a fever pitch, the atmosphere within the mission headquarters became charged with tension. Zara's attempts to quell the suspicions fell on deaf ears, the shadows of doubt proving stubbornly resilient. The sense of betrayal weighed heavily on her shoulders, yet she couldn't fathom that those closest to her could entertain the idea that she might be the architect of her own downfall.

Meanwhile, Thalia reveled in the chaos she had orchestrated. The sinister transformation within her was palpable, a darkness that eclipsed her former self. Her obsession with the ominous prophecy had morphed into a twisted conviction that she alone held the key to preventing an impending catastrophe. The power she wielded over the minds of others fueled her descent into madness, making her a formidable adversary, blinded by her warped sense of purpose.

The ominous undercurrents now threatened to drown the once-clear waters of camaraderie, casting a pall over the impending mission. Unable to comprehend the betrayal of those she held dear, Zara stood at the precipice of a growing storm, unaware of the tempest that would soon shatter the bonds that once bound her allies together.

As concerns for Zara's well-being burgeoned among her closest allies, a clandestine meeting unfolded in the quiet recesses of the UIA headquarters. Unified by their shared worry, leaders, mentors, and friends gathered to deliberate the gravity of the situation. The holographic displays of Eurydice, once a symbol of shared dreams, now flickered with uncertainty as they grappled with the rising influence of Thalia's ominous visions.

The air in the meeting room was thick with tension, the gravity of the situation pressing upon each participant. A holographic representation of Thalia's foreboding prophecies loomed over them, casting an eerie glow that mirrored the growing shadows of doubt. Here, the UIA decision-makers sought to confront the storm that threatened to shatter the unity forged through years of collaboration.

In a solemn procession, Zara was summoned to the meeting. The room, usually a strategic planning hub, now echoed with hushed tones of apprehension. The leaders, mentors, and friends who once stood firmly in Zara's corner now regarded her with searching eyes, assessing the veracity of the accusations that had tarnished her reputation.

The meeting became a crucible of emotions as Zara faced a barrage of questions, her loyalty and commitment scrutinized under the unforgiving gaze of those who had once championed her cause. The holographic displays flickered with each impassioned defense she presented, mirroring the instability of the situation at hand.

The dimly lit UIA meeting room hummed with tension as Zara stood before the assembled leaders, her usual air of confidence replaced by a sense of vulnerability. Chancellor Reynolds, the head of the UIA, leaned forward, his gaze piercing as he began the interrogation.

Chancellor Reynolds: Zara, these allegations are grave. The whispers suggest that your commitment to the Eurydice mission might be compromised. Can you address these concerns?

Zara, her jaw set with determination, responded: Chancellor, I have dedicated my entire career to this mission. There is no truth to these allegations. I am fully committed, and my loyalty to the UIA and the exploration of Eurydice remains unwavering.

Vice Admiral Rodriguez, a long-time mentor of Zara, raised a skeptical eyebrow: Zara, we've seen the holographic evidence presented by Thalia. It paints a disturbing picture. Can you explain your relationship with her and the nature of these visions?

Her eyes locked onto Vice Admiral Rodriguez's; Zara replied: Thalia and I were childhood friends. I had no knowledge of these visions until recently.

I am as baffled by them as you are. My focus has always been on the success of this mission.

Director Chen, a seasoned diplomat known for her keen insight, leaned forward: Zara, your friends, and mentors initiated an intervention with Thalia. Yet, she claims divine guidance. How do you explain this stark divergence in perspectives?

Zara, her voice tinged with frustration, answered: Thalia has changed. The intervention was an attempt to bring her back to reason, but she is convinced of an impending danger. I cannot control her beliefs, but my dedication to the mission remains steadfast.

Secretary-General Ramirez, a respected figure in the diplomatic community, interjected: Zara, it's not just Thalia's influence. There are concerns about your ability to lead amidst these accusations. How do you plan to navigate this turbulence?

Zara, with a steely resolve, asserted: I understand the gravity of the situation. I am willing to cooperate fully with any investigation. My commitment to this mission is unwavering, and I am confident that the truth will prevail.

As the questions continued, Zara's impassioned defense clashed against the skepticism of the UIA leaders. The holographic displays, reflecting the turmoil of the room, flickered in response to each charged exchange. The crucible of emotions intensified, leaving Zara acutely aware that the outcome of this investigation would shape not only her destiny but also the fate of the mission to Eurydice.

In a pivotal moment, the leaders of the UIA debated the unthinkable – whether Zara, their chosen leader, should continue to spearhead the mission or if the shadows of suspicion warranted a change in command. The weight of the decision reverberated through the room, and the once-unbreakable bonds that had tied Zara to her allies were now hung by a fragile thread.

As Zara concluded her testimony before the UIA, the room fell into a momentary silence, punctuated only by the soft hum of holographic displays. The weight of her words lingered in the air as the leaders retreated into the realm of deliberations. Left to contemplate the uncertainty of her future, Zara found herself walking the corridors in wonder. The echoes of her impassioned defense reverberated, mingling with the shadows of doubt that clung to the walls, creating a surreal landscape where the destiny of the Eurydice mission hung in the balance.

In the wake of the intense UIA meeting, the air hung heavy with uncertainty as Zara navigated the corridors of the headquarters. The holographic displays that had once symbolized her dreams of Eurydice now seemed to flicker with an uncertain glow. As the whispers of doubt lingered, a decision emerged from the crucible of scrutiny.

After careful consideration, Chancellor Reynolds addressed Zara with a measured tone: "Zara, the UIA acknowledges your longstanding commitment and contributions to the Eurydice mission. However, we have decided on a compromise in light of the concerns raised. You will continue to lead, but your leadership will be subject to ongoing reviews."

While not the complete exoneration Zara had hoped for, the verdict carried a glimmer of relief. She would be allowed to continue steering the mission, but the specter of further reviews loomed overhead. The organization that she had dedicated her life to had, for the moment, decided to extend a lifeline, albeit with strings attached.

As Zara grappled with the mixed emotions of gratitude and lingering uncertainty, she knew her journey to Eurydice was far from a smooth trajectory. The somber pall that had settled over her began to lift slightly, revealing a path fraught with challenges and a destiny that remained precariously balanced. The decision of the UIA was a temporary reprieve, leaving the mission and Zara's role in it teetering on the edge of a precipice.

The conclusion of the meeting left Zara in a state of bewilderment. Though not final, the verdict cast a somber pall over her as she grappled with the realization that the organization she had dedicated her life to was contemplating her removal. The long shadows of uncertainty lingered in the room, foreshadowing a looming battle. This battle extended beyond the exploration of Eurydice and delved into the heart of loyalty, trust, and the fragile nature of human bonds.

Thalia, seething with resentment and fueled by her ominous visions, regarded the UIA's decision to allow Zara to continue leading the Eurydice mission with a dark satisfaction. In the depths of her thoughts, a tempest of conflicting emotions churned, fueled by a brew of envy, bitterness, and a foreboding sense of destiny. As she delved into the recesses of her own consciousness, Thalia grappled with the complex tapestry of emotions that wove through the fabric of her existence.

The cosmic visions that had once been a shared dream with Zara now served as an unwelcome companion, whispering ominous prophecies that fueled Thalia's growing resentment. Each step Zara took on her cosmic journey felt like a delay in the inevitable clash that Thalia believed was destined to unfold. The dark satisfaction she derived from the UIA's decision was a bitter salve to the wounds of a once-unbreakable bond.

In the quiet moments of introspection, Thalia traced the threads of fate that had woven them together and marveled at destiny's cruel turns. The envy that gnawed at her core fueled a determination to disrupt the cosmic equilibrium, convinced that the UIA's decision was a flaw in the cosmic design that needed correction.

As Zara continued her cosmic odyssey, Thalia's thoughts became a battleground where the forces of darkness sought to manipulate her actions. Her dark satisfaction was a mask for the deeper turmoil within — a struggle against the malevolent forces that had subtly entwined her destiny with shadows. The ominous prophecies echoed in her mind, guiding her actions with a sense of inevitability that only fueled her determination to alter the course of cosmic destinies. Little did Thalia realize that her dark satisfaction was a mere prelude to the cosmic clash that loomed on the horizon, threatening to shatter the fragile bonds that once united them in a shared dream.

The Journey to Eurydice

Eurydice was named after a character from Greek mythology. Eurydice was a remote, rocky world located in a distant corner of the galaxy, beyond the reach of most known star systems. It was identified by UIA astronomers as a potential site for scientific research and exploration due to its unique geological features and the possibility of finding rare minerals and resources.

Eurydice's environment was harsh and unforgiving, with a barren, rocky surface scorched by intense radiation from the nearby star. The planet's atmosphere was thin and toxic, with high levels of sulfuric acid and other harmful gases. Eurydice had no liquid water on its surface, and its extreme temperatures ranged from sweltering during the day to freezing at night.

Despite these inhospitable conditions, the UIA believed that Eurydice could hold vital clues to the universe's origins and the evolution of planetary systems. Scientists hoped to study the planet's geology and mineralogy, searching for evidence of ancient volcanic activity, tectonic activity, and precious metals and minerals.

Explorers were also intrigued by the possibility of finding new life forms on the planet's surface or in its subsurface aquifers. Eurydice's extreme environment, with its intense radiation, sulfuric acid, and lack of liquid water, made the possibility of finding life forms even more intriguing. The UIA had equipped Zara's team with advanced instruments and technology, including drones, rovers, and geological probes, to help them explore the planet's surface and subsurface and collect data and samples.

Zara and her team understood the challenges of exploring Eurydice, but they were excited to make new discoveries and push the boundaries of human knowledge. They carefully planned their mission, taking into account the extreme conditions and the need to conserve resources. They knew their success would depend on their expertise, teamwork, and courage in the face of adversity.

Eurydice was located in a remote corner of the galaxy, thousands of light-years away from Earth. Zara and her team had to travel aboard the UIA's most advanced starship, the UESS Voyager, to reach the planet. The Voyager was a state-of-the-art vessel equipped with the latest technology, including a hyperdrive engine capable of traveling faster than the speed of light.

The journey to Eurydice took several months, even at the speed of the hyperdrive engine. Zara's crew comprised fifteen highly trained and experienced officers, including scientists, engineers, and medical personnel. They were carefully selected for their skills, knowledge, and ability to work effectively as a team.

The journey to Eurydice was uneventful, and the crew spent most of their time conducting routine maintenance and training exercises. They were all excited about exploring the planet and making new discoveries.

As they approached Eurydice, however, they received an unexpected signal from the planet's surface. It was a distress signal in the Terran Empire code. The crew was surprised to learn that Eurydice was not uninhabited, as they had expected, but instead was occupied by the Terran Empire.

Zara and her crew were shocked by the discovery and realized that their mission had suddenly become much more complicated. They quickly went on high alert and began to assess the situation. They knew they had to proceed cautiously, as any misstep could lead to a conflict with the Terran Empire.

The crew of the Voyager had to rethink their approach and adapt to the new reality of their mission. They had to balance their scientific curiosity with the need to respect the territorial rights of the Terran Empire. They also had to be prepared for the possibility of encountering hostile forces while remaining open to peaceful interaction and cooperation.

Zara knew her team was not trained for battle and would be disadvantaged if they encountered hostile forces on Eurydice. However, she also knew that they couldn't afford to be unprepared. So, as soon as they received the distress signal from Eurydice, she immediately called a meeting of her team to discuss the situation.

In their spacecraft's dimly lit briefing room, Zara gathered her team around the holographic table, the glow casting a subdued ambiance on their faces. The air was charged with urgency as Zara addressed her team, acknowledging the stark reality of the distress signal they had just received from Eurydice.

Zara, her expression a mix of determination and concern, leaned forward, her voice steady and commanding: "Team, I know we didn't sign up for a military mission, but Eurydice is unpredictable, and we need to be prepared for anything. Our training may not have been focused on combat, but we can't afford to be caught off guard."

The holographic representation of Eurydice shimmered in the center of the table, a stark reminder of the unknown dangers that awaited them. Zara continued, "We are not soldiers but trained professionals. Each one of you has skills and knowledge that go beyond the ordinary. We need to leverage that expertise to navigate whatever challenges lie ahead."

She emphasized the importance of maintaining composure in the face of danger, urging her team to stay calm and focused. "Fear is natural, but how we handle it defines us," Zara asserted. "Remember, we are a team. We've faced challenges before and always come out stronger on the other side. Eurydice is uncharted territory, but together, we have the resilience and adaptability to confront the unknown."

Zara's words resonated in the quiet room, each team member absorbing the gravity of the situation. The holographic display flickered, casting a dynamic light on their faces as they processed the weight of their mission. At that moment, Zara's leadership became a beacon of reassurance, guiding her team through the shadows of uncertainty that loomed over their journey to Eurydice.

Zara emphasized the importance of staying calm and focused when facing danger. She reminded her team that they were all trained professionals and had the skills and knowledge necessary to handle whatever challenges they might face.

Zara also ensured her team could access Voyager's weapons and defensive systems. She assigned each member of the team a specific role in case of an attack, even the scientists who were not used to combat situations.

Zara also ensured the team had plenty of supplies, including food, water, and medical equipment. She knew they might be stranded on the planet for an extended period, so she ensured they were well-equipped to handle any situation.

Finally, Zara emphasized the importance of teamwork and communication. She stressed that they needed to work together and support each other, even if they were not accustomed to working in combat situations. She also made sure that everyone was aware of the risks and the potential consequences of their actions.

Zara's team was ready for whatever lay ahead. Despite being scientists, they had been trained to work in high-pressure situations, but were they ready to face the challenges of this unexpected mission?

Zara and her team prepared for the landing as the Voyager approached Eurydice. They knew they were entering an unknown and potentially dangerous situation, so they took all necessary precautions.

The landing site must be chosen carefully to avoid potential hazards or obstacles. The team carefully analyzed the terrain of Eurydice from orbit and selected a relatively flat area free of any significant geological formations or potential dangers.

As the spacecraft descended towards the surface of Eurydice, the anticipation among Zara's team was palpable. Each member meticulously checked their equipment, ensuring every piece of advanced scanning technology was calibrated and ready for the crucial task ahead. The atmosphere inside the spacecraft was tense yet focused, the hum of machinery underscoring the gravity of their mission.

Zara, positioned at the forefront of the control center, monitored the descent with unwavering intensity. Once the landing protocols were initiated, the next crucial step in their operation unfolded: a comprehensive scan of the surrounding area. The success of their mission hinged on uncovering any potential threats or signs of life on Eurydice's enigmatic surface.

The team, comprised of specialists in various scientific disciplines, seamlessly transitioned into action. Advanced scanning equipment adorned the spacecraft's interior, each serving a distinct purpose in unraveling the mysteries of the uncharted planet. Sensors capable of detecting energy sources were activated, their delicate mechanisms finely tuned to pick up even the faintest signals that could signify life or potential dangers.

Devices designed to discern ground vibrations and movements sprang to life in tandem. The slightest tremor or disturbance would not escape their vigilant scrutiny, ensuring the team remained acutely aware of their surroundings. Zara, her eyes flicking across the array of screens, guided her team with precision and expertise.

As they prepared to execute the final stage of the scan, specialized cameras were deployed. These cutting-edge devices could capture images in a spectrum beyond the visible light range. Zara understood the significance of this capability – it allowed them to unveil hidden details, potential threats, or perhaps signs of life that might elude conventional observation.

The spacecraft, now hovering over the enigmatic terrain of Eurydice, initiated a synchronized ballet of technology and expertise. The hum of machinery intensified, the air thick with the tension of the unknown. Zara's leadership steered the team through the delicate dance of exploration, their advanced scanning equipment poised to unlock the secrets concealed within the alien landscape.

As they performed their scans, Zara's team remained vigilant and cautious, knowing that the enemy could be hiding just beyond their detection range. They scanned the area multiple times, covering every inch of the surrounding landscape.

Despite their efforts, however, they found no signs of life or enemy activity. The scans showed no energy signatures or movements in the ground, and the cameras revealed only Eurydice's barren, lifeless terrain.

Zara and her team knew this was a sign that the Terran Empire was highly skilled in stealth and deception. Their mission to explore Eurydice had suddenly become much more dangerous, and they would have to use all their skills and training to stay one step ahead of their foes.

The Voyager's engines roared as they approached the planet's surface, and Zara could feel the ship shuddering slightly as it made its way through the planet's atmosphere. She made sure that her team was strapped in and ready for impact.

As the Voyager touched the planet's surface, Zara could feel the ship's landing gear engage with the ground. There was a loud thud, and the ship came to a stop. Everything was silent momentarily as the team waited to ensure they had landed safely.

After a few moments, Zara gave the all-clear, and the team began the process of disembarking from the Voyager. They were immediately struck by the eerie silence of the planet, which was a stark contrast to the bustling atmosphere of the ship they had just left.

As Zara and her team disembarked from their spacecraft, she couldn't help but feel a sense of anxiety creeping up on her. This was her first time in a potential battle, and the prospect of facing off against the Terran Empire, a known and powerful enemy, was daunting.

Zara knew that she had to overcome her anxiety if she was going to lead her team effectively. She reminded herself of the countless hours she had spent training and preparing for this moment. She recalled the challenges she had overcome in her career and the obstacles she had faced and overcome.

She also reminded herself of the importance of their mission. They were not just exploring Eurydice for the sake of exploration. They were there to expand the boundaries of human knowledge and to make a valuable contribution to the scientific community. Their mission was too important to be derailed by anxiety or fear.

Zara took a deep breath, squared her shoulders, and stepped off the spacecraft onto the barren terrain of Eurydice. As she did, she felt a sense of purpose and determination wash over her. She knew she had a responsibility to her team and the mission, and she was determined to see it through.

The moment the airlock hissed open, Zara led her team onto the unfamiliar surface of Eurydice. A hushed anticipation hung in the thin, metallic-tasting air, a tangible reminder of the unexplored planet's unique atmosphere. The team, clad in their advanced exploration suits, stepped cautiously onto the alien terrain, their movements deliberate and synchronized.

The landscape stretched before them, a panorama of alien vistas bathed in an otherworldly light. Zara's eyes, shielded by her visor, scanned the surroundings as her boots made contact with the foreign soil. The crunch of Eurydice's surface beneath her feet echoed through the team's communication channels, a rhythmic reminder of the historic moment they were collectively experiencing.

Setting up their equipment with practiced efficiency, the team created a temporary base camp to serve as the hub for their scientific endeavors. Arrays of advanced sensors were strategically placed, capturing data on atmospheric composition, temperature variations, and electromagnetic fields. Each piece of equipment hummed with activity, extending the team's reach into the mysteries of Eurydice.

As the team initiated their exploratory tasks, Zara's leadership shone through. She directed the deployment of autonomous drones equipped with specialized sensors to survey the immediate vicinity and gather information beyond the reach of human exploration. The drones whirred into action, their propellers cutting through the thin Eurydician air as they transmitted real-time data back to the base camp.

The team, each member assigned specific tasks, delved into their roles purposefully. Scientists wielded handheld analyzers, their eyes glued to digital displays as they deciphered the composition of Eurydice's soil and the unique signatures of its rocks. Biologists, equipped with portable containment units, carefully collected samples of the planet's flora, if any existed.

Amidst the scientific fervor, Zara took a moment to gaze at the expansive horizon, her visor reflecting the alien landscape. The thin atmosphere held a promise of discoveries yet to be unveiled, and the metallic taste lingered as a reminder of the planet's distinct identity. The team, propelled by a collective passion for exploration, embarked on a journey into the unknown, their experiments and readings laying the groundwork for unraveling the secrets concealed within Eurydice's uncharted terrain.

In the grip of mounting anxiety, Zara fought to maintain focus and alertness as their exploration of the alien planet unfolded. With each step into the unknown, her heart raced, an uneasy undercurrent of tension threading through her every decision. Despite the internal turmoil, Zara projected an outward facade of confidence and authority, drawing strength from her training and experience to guide her team through the disquieting terrain.

Yet, the initial excitement accompanying their arrival on Eurydice soon withered into a palpable sense of unease. The alien landscape, bathed in an otherworldly light, now seemed to cast elongated shadows that danced with the uncertainties ahead.

The tension escalated when another urgent distress signal from the Terran Empire pierced the already fraught atmosphere.

The spacecraft's communication system crackled to life, cutting through the ambient hum of instruments and the distant whispers of Eurydice's winds. The urgency in the distress signal from the Terran Empire was palpable, a digital cry for help that echoed through the spacecraft's confines and reverberated in the anxious hearts of Zara and her team.

The message, laden with desperation, carried the weight of a civilization grappling with unforeseen calamity. The once-familiar voice from the Terran Empire, now strained and fraught, painted a vivid picture of a situation teetering on the brink of disaster. Zara, her gaze fixed on the holographic display, absorbed the distressing details — a settlement imperiled, lives hanging in the balance, and a plea for assistance that resonated across the cosmic void.

As the distress signal unfolded, the sense of peril permeated the spacecraft like a shadow, casting a somber pall over the once hopeful atmosphere of exploration. Feeling the gravity of the situation, Zara grappled with the moral imperative to respond. The connection between Earth and the Terran Empire was a lifeline stretching across the vast expanse of space, and Zara couldn't turn a blind eye to the call for help, even in the face of their own precarious circumstances on Eurydice.

The intricate dance of responsibility and uncertainty played out in Zara's mind. The plight of the Terran Empire tugged at her sense of duty, compelling her to consider the broader implications of their mission. The decision to explore Eurydice, once driven by scientific curiosity, now intersected with the moral imperative to aid a fellow settlement in distress.

As Zara addressed her team, the unease that had settled over them transformed into a shared sense of determination. They couldn't ignore the call for help; it resonated with the very essence of their humanity. The distress signal became a rallying point, a juncture where the boundaries of exploration and duty blurred, forging a new path fraught with uncertainty but guided by the resilient spirit of humanity.

The message, fraught with desperation, conveyed a clear sense that the Empire was ensnared in a perilous situation. Zara's anxiety deepened as the weight of the distress signal settled upon her shoulders. She knew they were venturing into uncharted realms fraught with potential danger, and she felt the burden of responsibility to prepare her team for the ominous challenges ahead.

In the midst of this swirling anxiety, Zara, drawing on a reserve of inner strength, began to ease the tension. Though still tinged with concern, her voice carried a thread of reassurance as she briefed her team on the gravity of the situation. Little did they know that the distress signal would plunge them into a cascade of uncertainties that would test their mettle in ways they could never have anticipated.

Echoes of Deception

As Zara and her crew closed in on the coordinates of the distress signal, an ominous sight awaited them in the cosmic expanse. A massive spaceship, its sleek metallic contours catching the distant light of Eurydice's alien sun, hung ominously in the sky. The initial moments were shrouded in uncertainty as the team, their anticipation veiled by the unknown, struggled to discern the identity of the colossal vessel.

The spaceship, surrounded by an aura of mystery, reflected the hues of Eurydice's enigmatic atmosphere.

The interplay of shadows on the spaceship's surface added an air of ambiguity, making it challenging to determine its origin or allegiance. Zara's trained eyes swept over the colossal craft, searching for clues, yet the enigma persisted. The absence of clear identification set the stage for a suspenseful encounter, leaving the team on the precipice of discovery and uncertainty.

As they cautiously approached, the formidable silhouette of the unknown spaceship loomed larger, casting an ominous shadow over the team's mission. The distress signal, seemingly originating from this colossal enigma, had drawn them into a cosmic conundrum, and the void of information intensified the gravity of the situation. Little did they know that the next moments would unravel a sinister plot, revealing a threat far more insidious than the call for help they had initially perceived.

As Zara and crew approached the colossal vessel hanging ominously in the Eurydician sky, an unsettling realization rippled through the team. The enigmatic spaceship's lack of discernible markings or identifiers cast a pall of uncertainty over the unfolding situation. Zara's instincts, honed through years of exploration and leadership, tingled with caution.

Gathering her team around the central console, Zara's voice cut through the tense atmosphere, "We can't proceed blindly into this unknown. The absence of identification raises too many questions. We need to exercise caution and prioritize our safety."

The team's expressions, reflecting a mix of anticipation and apprehension, acknowledged the gravity of the situation. The spacecraft, its metallic surface gleaming in the eerie light of Eurydice, seemed to pulse with an inscrutable energy. The distress signal, which had initially beckoned them toward a humanitarian mission, now cloaked itself in the shadows of ambiguity.

Zara, her gaze fixed on the colossal vessel through the observation deck, made the decisive call, "Initiate evasive maneuvers. We'll find cover behind one of Eurydice's larger rock formations. We can't risk exposing ourselves until we know more about the origin and intent of that ship."

As the spacecraft altered its trajectory, seeking refuge behind the natural cover of the alien planet, a sense of vulnerability settled over the team. The unknown vessel loomed in the periphery, a silent sentinel in the cosmic expanse. The decision to seek cover was not just a tactical move but a strategic response to the unfolding enigma that threatened to engulf them.

The team, their movements purposeful and coordinated, worked in unison to navigate the spacecraft to safety. Zara, her gaze never wavering from the mysterious craft, felt the weight of responsibility settle on her shoulders. The decision to seek cover was a testament to her commitment to the safety of her team, a calculated response to the veiled threat that hovered in the vastness of space.

As the spacecraft nestled behind the protective embrace of Eurydice's rock formations, the enigma of the colossal vessel continued to cast its shadow. Her mind racing with possibilities and uncertainties, Zara prepared her team for the next phase – a meticulous investigation to unravel the secrets concealed within the metallic contours of the unknown spacecraft.

The need for shelter was palpable. The energy emanating from the colossal vessel was powerful, its unseen force creating a pull that hinted at dangers beyond their current understanding. Trusting her instincts honed through years of cosmic exploration, Zara sensed that exposure to this unknown energy could threaten both their technology and their well-being. The decision to seek cover was not just a precautionary measure; it was a response to an intuitive understanding that some cosmic forces were best approached with caution and from the safety of the shadows. Despite the urgency, the team moved with precision, finding refuge behind Eurydice's rock formations, shielded from the enigmatic vessel's gaze.

Quickly, Zara and her team looked for additional cover. Zara knew she had to find a safer place to regroup and plan her next move. Time was of the essence. Using her advanced terrain knowledge and survival skills, she scoured the area, searching for a suitable shelter.

As the team maneuvered behind the rock formations, Zara's sharp eyes scanned the surroundings, seeking a location that offered both concealment and strategic advantage. The vast expanse of Eurydice's landscape stretched before them, an alien terrain that held both mystery and potential danger.

Finally, she stumbled upon an abandoned bunker that was hidden from view behind a rocky outcrop. The door was rusted and difficult to open, but with her strength and determination, Zara managed to pry it open. The creaking sound echoed through the stillness of Eurydice, a testament to the age of the structure and the secrets it might hold.

As the team entered the bunker, a dim light flickered to life, revealing a corridor that led deeper into the underground complex. The air inside was stale, a testament to years of abandonment. Zara's mind raced with possibilities as she assessed the surroundings. The bunker seemed to be a relic from a bygone era, its purpose shrouded in the cosmic mysteries surrounding Eurydice.

With a commanding tone, Zara instructed her team to secure the entrance. As the team exited to secure the bunker's entrance, Zara, with a resolute determination, decided to stay behind momentarily. The holographic displays bathed the underground chamber in an otherworldly glow as she continued to sift through the data acquired from the celestial archives. The enigmatic symbols on the walls seemed to pulse with an unseen energy, and Zara felt an inexplicable connection to the cosmic revelations.

"Stay vigilant," she instructed her team as they geared up to secure the area outside. "We need to be prepared for whatever awaits us. We can't afford to underestimate the potential threats Eurydice holds."

Armed with advanced technology and a sense of purpose, her team filed out of the bunker, leaving Zara alone in the subterranean chamber. The door creaked shut behind them, sealing Zara in a cocoon of ancient mysteries and futuristic technology.

Zara's focus intensified as the echoes of her team's footsteps faded. The holographic displays flickered with new information, and her mind delved deeper into the cosmic tapestry she had uncovered. The revelations were both mesmerizing and confounding, and Zara found herself at the nexus of knowledge and uncertainty.

Outside the bunker, her team spread out, scanning the surroundings for any signs of activity. The metallic surface of the unknown vessel gleamed in the ambient light, an imposing presence against the alien landscape. Little did they know that the shadows of the Terran Empire's impending arrival lurked beyond the horizon, poised to shatter the fragile peace that Eurydice once offered.

Unbeknownst to Zara, the cosmic forces at play converged, weaving a narrative that transcended the boundaries of time and space. As her team prepared to secure the area, the impending clash with the Terran Empire loomed on the horizon, an ominous storm gathering strength in the cosmic abyss.

As she stepped deeper inside the bunker, her heart racing, she felt relief wash over her. The bunker was spacious and well-equipped, with a generator, a communication system, and enough supplies to last several weeks.

At the same time, Zara couldn't help but feel a twinge of suspicion and curiosity. Who had built this bunker, and why had they abandoned it? Were there others on this planet, or was this just a lone structure in an otherwise desolate landscape?

Eurydice had been thought to be a supposedly uninhabitable planet. Zara's head was spinning; she couldn't help but feel a mixture of surprise and relief. The fact that such a well-equipped and spacious shelter existed on this seemingly barren and lifeless planet was a revelation.

Zara's training kicked in as her thoughts raced, reminding her to focus on the immediate task. She needed to secure the bunker and establish a communication link with nearby allies. She quickly set to work, surveying the area for signs of enemy activity and fortifying the bunker's defenses.

However, despite her best efforts to remain calm and rational, Zara couldn't shake off the feeling of unease that had settled in the pit of her stomach. The discovery of the bunker opened up new possibilities but also raised many more questions and uncertainties. She knew she had to tread carefully and be prepared for whatever lay ahead.

As Zara huddled in the safety of the abandoned bunker, she saw the massive spaceship slowly descending from the sky. The ship was colossal, easily the size of a small city, with a gleaming metallic exterior that shone in the bright sunlight. Its sheer size was overwhelming, casting a looming shadow over the surrounding landscape.

As the spaceship got closer, Zara could see the intricate details on its surface. Whirling lights and flashing panels covered the entire vessel's length, creating a mesmerizing effect. The air around them was disturbed by the sheer force of the engines, causing a deafening noise that made it difficult for Zara and her team to communicate.

Suddenly, a dust cloud rose from the ground as the spaceship landed, settling around it like a shroud. Zara felt her heart pounding in her chest as she realized this was not just any spaceship but a vessel from the Terran Empire. Her years of training had prepared her for this moment, but she could feel the anxiety rising within her as she knew that this encounter could lead to devastating consequences.

The vessel's emblem, a menacing black eagle with wings outstretched, was emblazoned on the ship's side, leaving no doubt about its origins. The emblem's revelation left Zara and her team in awe, contemplating the possibility of an advanced cloaking device that had concealed the vessel's identity until this critical moment. The once-invisible emblem now served as a chilling declaration of the unknown ship's origin, instilling a renewed sense of foreboding among the team. Zara knew the Terran Empire was a formidable opponent, and their mere presence on Eurydice threatened her team's safety.

From the vantage point of the rocky bunker, Zara's eyes widened as the colossal ship's hatch opened with a low, ominous hum. A ramp, hidden beneath the vessel's sleek surface, unfurled like a metallic tongue, connecting the alien craft to the unforgiving terrain of Eurydice. The once-veiled soldiers, clad in formidable black armor adorned with the menacing emblem of the black eagle, descended the ramp with an eerie precision.

Dim blue lights embedded along the ramp's edges cast an otherworldly glow that revealed the soldiers' stoic expressions. The cold metallic echoes of their boots reverberated in the alien silence as they formed a disciplined formation on the barren ground. Each soldier, a silent sentinel against the alien backdrop, carried an air of efficiency that belied the enigma of their true purpose on Eurydice.

As Zara observed from the safety of the bunker, a shiver ran down her spine. The emergence of the soldiers, orchestrated with almost mechanical precision, heightened the tension in the air. The lights along the ramp flickered intermittently, casting fleeting shadows over the soldiers' ominous figures. The black eagle emblem, now visible on their armor, seemed to pulsate with unsettling energy, mirroring the mystery surrounding their sudden appearance on the uncharted planet.

The soldiers, their faces obscured by the shadows of their helmets, moved with an unsettling unity that suggested a shared purpose. Zara, her instincts on high alert, couldn't shake the feeling that the unfolding scenario held consequences far beyond the scope of their initial mission. As the soldiers fanned out, surveying the alien landscape with an intensity that mirrored the unknown, the stage was set for a confrontation that would unveil the true nature of their enigmatic visitors.

Around a dozen of them were marching in a disciplined and organized formation, their shiny metal armor reflecting the harsh sunlight.

The soldiers wore sleek, black battle suits that covered them from head to toe. The suits were adorned with sophisticated weaponry and gadgets, each soldier carrying a formidable array of advanced technology that made it clear they were not to be underestimated.

Their helmets were sleek and angular, hiding their faces behind a layer of opaque glass. Zara couldn't help but feel a sense of foreboding as she watched the soldiers move with an almost robotic precision, their movements calculated and deliberate.

She knew that these soldiers represented the Terran Empire and that they were the enemy. Zara steeled herself for the battle ahead, determined to defend the bunker and its secrets from these invaders.

Sheltered within the confines of the rocky bunker, Zara cast her discerning gaze across the dark interior, its walls bearing the scars of time and history etched into the Eurydician rock. The bunker, a relic of a bygone era, held secrets of explorers who had ventured into the cosmos long before her. Dust-covered equipment and faded holographic displays spoke of past missions, their successes, and challenges embedded in the very fabric of the shelter. Yet, as her eyes scanned the chamber, a realization dawned – the bunker, steeped in history, offered no solace in weaponry or defenses. It stood as a testament to the curiosity of those who came before. Still, in the face of the enigmatic soldiers outside, it became clear that their arsenal of knowledge would be the only shield Zara could wield in this uncharted confrontation on Eurydice.

Suddenly, amidst the dusty relics and echoes of exploration within the bunker, Zara's searching gaze fell upon a concealed compartment. She activated a hidden panel with a cautious touch, revealing a technology that surpassed anything the UIA had ever encountered. A holographic interface materialized, displaying intricate schematics of an advanced defense mechanism. This cutting-edge technology, a marvel that surpassed the boundaries of known exploration, held the potential to change the tides of their predicament.

As Zara delved into the holographic interface, she realized that this advanced defense system was a creation of the bunker's original explorers, a safeguard against unforeseen threats in the cosmos. The UIA had never been privy to such ingenuity, and the implications of this discovery weighed heavily on Zara's shoulders. The intricate network of energy shields, stealth capabilities, and various defensive mechanisms surpassed any weapon in the UIA's arsenal.

Zara and her team didn't have weeks to pour over the information, analyze and decipher the advanced technology and theories; they had scant moments. They could recognize new technologies that could revolutionize space travel and energy production and insights into the universe's origins and the nature of reality itself.

Zara knew that if the Terran Empire got their hands on this knowledge, they would have an insurmountable advantage over the UIA and potentially the entire galaxy. That's why she was willing to risk everything to protect the secrets of the bunker and the knowledge it contained.

Despite the danger, Zara decided to lead her team by leaving the safety of the bunker and facing the soldiers head-on with her crew. She knew they were outnumbered and outgunned, but she couldn't let fear or hesitation cloud her judgment.

As she gathered her team and prepared them for battle, Zara's mind raced with the possibilities and consequences of their actions. She knew that the outcome of this fight could have far-reaching implications, not just for their mission but for the galaxy's future.

But despite all these thoughts swirling in her mind, Zara remained focused on the task. She was responsible for protecting the secrets of the bunker and her team, and she was determined to do whatever it took to fulfill that responsibility.

With a deep breath, Zara led her team out of and towards the waiting soldiers of the Terran Empire, her heart pounding with a mixture of fear and resolve.

The slaughter was brutal and swift. Zara and her team were caught off-guard as even more soldiers of the Terran Empire stormed out of their ship and opened fire. The laser beams they unleashed were deadly accurate and powerful, tearing through the air with a high-pitched whine and striking the ground with explosive force. The UIA team tried to take cover behind the rocks and boulders that surrounded them, but it was no use. The soldiers were too numerous and too well-equipped. They moved with cold efficiency, their armor and weapons gleaming in the setting sun's light.

Zara watched in horror as her team was cut down before her eyes. She could hear the screams and cries of her comrades as they fell to the ground, their bodies torn apart by the lethal beams of energy. The air was filled with the acrid smell of burning flesh and ozone. Zara tried to fight back, firing her own laser pistol at the soldiers, but it was like trying to stop a tidal wave with a bucket. The soldiers were simply too powerful, too well-trained, and too well-equipped. In a matter of seconds, it was all over.

Zara was the only one left standing, her heart pounding in her chest as she looked around at the carnage that surrounded her. The soldiers of the Terran Empire had accomplished their mission, wiping out the UIA team.

But they had yet to claim the secrets of the bunker for themselves.

Zara managed to dodge the attack and escape into the safety of the bunker, but she knew that this was just the beginning of a long and brutal war.

Zara quickly realized that they had fallen into a trap. The distress signal was a deception to lure them into a deadly ambush.

Zara was devastated by the loss of her team, but she knew she had to act fast if she wanted to survive and avenge their deaths.

As Zara stood in the bunker, grappling with the weight of the discovery of advanced defense technology, an internal struggle waged within her. The holographic interface displayed a stark choice – to push the emergency beacon on her uniform, a small device that sent out a distress signal to any nearby ships or stations, alerting them to her situation, and activate the formidable defense system or to remain hidden, the potential consequences of her decision stretching far beyond the rocky confines of Eurydice.

On one hand, the implications of pushing the button weighed heavily on Zara's mind. The UIA, an organization built on exploration and cooperation, might view her response to the Terran Empire's distress signal as an act of aggression. The diplomatic repercussions were unfathomable, and the specter of tarnishing her lifelong dedication to the UIA haunted her thoughts. The delicate balance between loyalty to the organization and the moral imperative to protect herself danced on a precipice, leaving Zara tormented by the potential condemnation that might follow.

With a profound sense of resolve, Zara decided to push the emergency button. The holographic display responded with a cascade of illuminated indicators, activating the advanced defense system. The bunker's atmosphere crackled with the energy of an impending confrontation. The fate of her own life, the delicate equilibrium of diplomatic relations, and the protection of the groundbreaking technology all converged in this pivotal moment.

As the holographic interface hummed to life, Zara's heart pounded in sync with the events unfolding. The weight of her decision, a gamble against an uncertain future, rested on her shoulders. The button, once a symbol of an unwavering commitment to exploration, now became a beacon of defense and defiance.

As the seconds stretched into an eternity, Zara huddled in the bunker, the weight of her decision palpable in the charged air. The silence that followed the activation of the defense system echoed with anticipation, and the tension in the bunker was thick with uncertainty. Every passing moment felt like an eternity, the unknown consequences of her choice looming ominously.

Then, a distant hum broke through the stillness, and Zara's heart quickened. The sound of engines overhead heralded a group of ships descending from the alien sky, their silhouettes cutting through the ambient light. A mixture of relief and urgency flooded Zara as she realized it was her chance to escape the impending clash. The ships, a lifeline in the abyss of uncertainty, represented the possibility of evading the consequences of her decision and charting a course through the unknown expanse of Eurydice.

The UIA rescue team had arrived just in time and brought a fleet of small, nimble ships designed for quick strikes and maneuvers. As they flew in formation towards the Empire's ship, they opened fire, drawing the attention of the soldiers below.

The Empire's soldiers, trained to follow orders without question, focused on the incoming ships, firing their weapons toward them. The rescue team's ships responded with evasive maneuvers, dodging laser beams and returning fire.

Zara knew she could not get caught in the bunker, so she decided to escape despite the fighting around her. As she fled the bunker, Zara could hear the sound of boots pounding on the ground behind her. She knew she had to outmaneuver the Empire soldiers, who were surely chasing after her. She ran through the rocky terrain, taking sharp turns and jumping over boulders. Her heart was pounding in her chest, and her breath was ragged. Zara knew the Empire soldiers had superior weapons and technology, so she had to rely on her wit and cunning to escape. She quickly realized that the terrain was her advantage. The soldiers were trained to fight in open fields, and the rocky terrain would slow them down. As Zara ran, she noticed a narrow ravine up ahead. She knew it was risky, but she took the chance and veered towards it. She slid down the steep incline, barely managing to keep her balance. She knew the soldiers would have to slow down to navigate the narrow passage, giving her a precious few moments to gain distance. Zara continued running until she found a small crevice in the rocks. She squeezed into the tight space, hiding in the shadows. She could hear the soldiers' footsteps getting closer and closer, and her heart was pounding in her chest. The soldiers passed by her hiding spot, unaware of her presence.

Zara waited a few moments to ensure they were gone, then ran off again. She could feel the adrenaline pumping through her veins, her heart pounding. She knew that if she didn't move quickly, she would eventually be caught by the Empire's soldiers.

As she ran through the rocky terrain of Eurydice, Zara felt a deep sense of loss and sorrow for her fallen comrades. She knew that the Empire's deception had cost them their lives and that they had been sacrificed for the Empire's own gain.

Zara knew that she had to make it back to her own spacecraft and escape before the Empire could catch up to her. She ran with all her might, her heart pounding in her chest and her lungs burning with exhaustion. Zara realized the gravity of the situation they were in. Her team had been attacked and killed, and she was alone in a hostile environment, facing an enemy that was far more powerful and ruthless than she had ever imagined. She knew that she had to remain calm and focused if she was to survive and fight back against the Terran Empire.

As she reached her ship, she heard a loud explosion behind her. Glancing back, she saw that one of the rescue ships had been hit, and it was careening towards the ground. She could hear the screams of the pilots as they went down, and she knew that they had sacrificed themselves to give her a chance to escape.

With the taste of urgency still lingering, Zara swiftly ascended the ramp of her ship, her breaths echoing the rapid rhythm of her heart. The metallic hum of the engines responded to her commands as she expertly navigated the controls. The ship roared to life, a symphony of power and propulsion, and the ground beneath trembled as Zara prepared for liftoff. The moment of escape hung in the balance, and she felt the weight of the looming Empire ships pursuing her.

As the spacecraft ascended, the air became a frenetic blur, and Zara deftly maneuvered through the alien skies of Eurydice. The pursuing Empire ships relentlessly pursued and unleashed a barrage of laser fire that streaked through the atmosphere like fiery tendrils. Zara skillfully piloted her ship through the dazzling display of light, narrowly evading each laser's deadly trajectory.

The dance between pursuit and evasion unfolded in the cosmic theater, and Zara's senses were heightened as she weaved through the intricate ballet of danger. The turbulent sky became a canvas of uncertainty, and the adrenaline coursing through her veins fueled her determination to elude the relentless grasp of the Empire.

As the pursuing ships struggled to match the agility of Zara's spacecraft, she soared higher into the Eurydician sky, leaving the chaos of the pursuit behind. The triumphant hum of her ship's engines drowned out the distant echoes of laser fire, and Zara knew that this escape marked not only a victory against the Empire's pursuit but also the preservation of the groundbreaking technology and the lives of her team. The vast expanse of Eurydice unfolded beneath her, a canvas of unknown possibilities as she charted a course away from the conflict and towards an uncertain future in the cosmic tapestry of exploration.

With a final glance over her shoulder, Zara witnessed the unfolding chaos in the Eurydician sky. The imposing silhouette of the Terran Empire's ship, once a harbinger of danger, is now encircled by the defiant UIA rescue ships. The celestial arena transformed into a battleground as lasers streaked through the cosmos, creating an intricate tapestry of light and conflict.

The rescue ships, maneuvering with strategic precision, engaged the Empire vessel in a fierce dance of combat. Beams of energy crisscrossed the expanse, leaving trails of ephemeral brilliance in their wake. The metallic clangor of impacts reverberated through space, punctuating the symphony of battle that unfolded against the alien backdrop.

As Zara's ship hurtled through the cosmic void, the intensity of the conflict behind her painted a tableau of defiance against imperial aggression. The UIA rescue ships, driven by the same spirit of exploration that had initially united them, confronted the Terran Empire with a resolute determination. Each laser volley, each evasive maneuver, was a testament to the indomitable will of those who sought to protect the sanctity of their mission and the lives intertwined with the pursuit of knowledge.

The once-ominous Empire ship, now ensnared in the relentless onslaught of the UIA rescue fleet, became a spectacle of defiance against tyranny. The battle, a clash of ideologies echoing through the vastness of space, carried with it the weight of the decisions made on Eurydice. Zara, pressing forward into the unknown, knew that the outcome of this celestial confrontation would reverberate far beyond the confines of the battlefield, shaping the narrative of the cosmic journey that awaited them.

As she flew away from Eurydice, Zara couldn't help but wonder what the future held in store. The Empire's treachery had led to the loss of her team and the start of what would become known as the Great War. Zara knew she had to find a way to stop the Empire and prevent them from wreaking further havoc on the galaxy.

As Zara piloted her ship through the vast expanse of space, the enigma of the Terran Empire's awareness gnawed at the edges of her thoughts. Eurydice had been a closely guarded secret, a top-tier mission veiled in confidentiality. The realization that the Empire not only knew of their mission but actively sought to intervene left Zara grappling with an unsettling question – how had their clandestine expedition been exposed?

The pulsating hum of the ship's engines provided a dissonant backdrop to Zara's contemplation. She retraced the steps of their planning, the closed-door meetings, and the whispered conversations that had forged the path to Eurydice. The realization struck her like a meteor – someone within their inner circle had betrayed them, laying bare the details of the mission to the Empire.

Dread settled in the pit of Zara's stomach as she considered the implications. A sinking feeling hinted that the betrayal might be more personal than she initially thought. The tendrils of suspicion began to snake through her mind, circling around the faces of those who had been privy to the mission details. It was inconceivable that a breach of such magnitude could occur unless it came from someone intimately connected to the team.

Zara's intuition, honed through years of exploration, hinted that the betrayer might be closer than she dared to acknowledge.

The journey back to the UIA base became more than a physical return; it evolved into a quest for answers. The tendrils of betrayal unfurled, weaving a narrative that surpassed the cosmic exploration of Eurydice. The revelation awaiting Zara, tangled within the labyrinth of trust and treachery, would reshape the trajectory of their mission and the foundation of bonds that had once been unbreakable.

As a young cadet, Zara had dreamed of commanding her own starship and exploring the vast reaches of space. She had worked hard to earn her place in the UIA and had quickly risen through the ranks. But she knew that her path to command had not been easy, and it became tougher with the beginning of the Great War.

A Fresh Start

In the aftermath of the fierce battle with the Terran Empire, Zara returned to the solemn halls of the UIA headquarters, her steps echoing in the corridors that bore witness to the triumphs and tragedies of cosmic exploration. The scent of lingering sorrow hung in the air as she awaited the inevitable debriefing, her mind a tempest of emotions swirling with the memories of Eurydice.

Seated in a dimly lit room adorned with holographic displays, Zara faced a panel of UIA officials. Their expressions, a mix of scrutiny and contemplation, mirrored the gravity of the situation. The holographic displays flickered with images of the battleground, the clash with the Terran Empire vividly replaying before them. Zara's strategic maneuvers, the valiant sacrifice of the rescue ships, and the protective shield she had cast over the groundbreaking technology within the bunker—all laid bare for evaluation.

The air thickened as the superiors delved into the intricacies of her decisions. Each moment of the confrontation was dissected with precision, the sacrifices of her crew acknowledged with a solemn nod. Zara's resilience and selflessness in the face of insurmountable odds became the focal point of the discussion. The unanimous agreement resonated through the room – her actions safeguarded advanced technology and the future of UIA's cosmic endeavors.

The verdict was delivered in recognition of her unwavering commitment and the sacrifices she made. Zara's next assignment would take her to the outpost on Aurora Beta, a pivotal post on the fringes of known space. The mission: to monitor the movements of the Terran Empire, a task that aligned with her skills as a seasoned explorer and the need for a vigilant guardian on the cosmic frontier.

As the superiors relayed the assignment, a mix of emotions swept over Zara. The somber acknowledgment of the losses suffered, the weight of her newfound responsibility, and the unwavering resolve to honor the legacy of her fallen crew all converged within her. The journey to Aurora Beta became a bridge between the echoes of the past and the uncharted realms of the future. Here, the shadows of the Terran Empire would be met with the vigilant gaze of a steadfast explorer, determined to turn the page and forge a new chapter in the cosmic odyssey.

In the quiet aftermath of the meeting, Zara found herself alone with her thoughts. The weight of command settled on her shoulders, and the faces of her fallen crew haunted her every contemplation. The room, adorned with holographic projections of the recent battle, became a sanctuary for reflection.

A holographic projection displayed the vibrant image of Eurydice, a stark reminder of the price paid for their journey into the unknown. Zara couldn't escape the shadows of that ill-fated mission, the echoes of the Terran Empire's threat, and the sacrifice of her comrades. The holographic displays flickered like cosmic constellations, telling a tale of courage and loss.

In the following days, Zara prepared for her new assignment on Aurora Beta. The outpost on the fringes of known space stood as a frontier against the encroaching darkness. Her mission was clear, but the uncertainty of the cosmic expanse lay before her. The superiors, recognizing her strategic acumen and determination, had entrusted her with a pivotal role.

As the newly appointed guardian on the cosmic frontier, Zara felt the burden of responsibility and a spark of determination. The remnants of her crew's sacrifice fueled her resolve to stand against the looming threat of the Terran Empire. The journey to Aurora Beta became more than a relocation; it became a quest for redemption and a pledge to protect the future of cosmic exploration.

The transition to Aurora Beta marked a fresh start, not just for Zara but for the UIA. Perched on the edge of the cosmic unknown, the outpost would serve as a beacon of resistance against the encroaching darkness. The shadows of Eurydice lingered, but so did the indomitable spirit of exploration that had ignited Zara's journey.

As the spacecraft departed for the fringes of the cosmos, Zara looked back one last time at the UIA headquarters. The echoes of the past resonated in the corridors, and the weight of command felt both daunting and empowering. The cosmic odyssey continued, with Zara at the helm, determined to navigate the uncharted realms and safeguard the future of exploration from the shadows that sought to engulf it.

Aurora Beta

Aurora Beta, perched on the outer edges of known space, unfolded as a distant outpost amidst the cosmic canvas. The environment was stark and foreboding, with the distant glow of unfamiliar stars casting an ethereal luminescence across the alien landscape. The outpost, a testament to humanity's reach into the unknown, stood as a solitary structure against the cosmic tapestry, its metallic contours blending with the desolate terrain.

The headquarters on Aurora Beta, a labyrinthine structure with corridors that echoed the hushed whispers of exploration, became Zara's new command center. Its walls bore the marks of countless missions, each scar a testament to the relentless pursuit of knowledge in the face of cosmic uncertainty. The control room, adorned with holographic displays that flickered with data from the far reaches of space, served as the nerve center for monitoring the movements of the Terran Empire.

The crew assigned to Zara hailed from diverse backgrounds, each member a seasoned explorer with their own stories etched into the fabric of the cosmos. The air within the outpost was thick with a blend of anticipation and apprehension. The crew, aware of Zara's past and the shadows that clung to her, harbored a mixture of anxiety and respect. Whispers of her actions on Eurydice, the sacrifice of her team, and the confrontation with the Terran Empire lingered like phantoms in the collective consciousness of the crew.

Zara, acutely aware of the eyes that followed her every move, endeavored to bridge the gap between the echoes of the past and the collective purpose of their mission. She held briefings where the weight of her words sought to dispel the anxieties within the crew. The holographic displays illuminated with trajectories and intelligence reports, laying bare the cosmic chessboard they navigated.

The outpost, surrounded by the silent expanse of Aurora Beta, became a nexus of vigilance against the encroaching shadows of the Terran Empire.

Zara sat alone in the dimly lit command center of the UIA outpost on Aurora Beta, her thoughts racing back to the battle on Eurydice. She couldn't shake the memories of her fallen team, their lifeless bodies scattered around. Her heart ached as she remembered the brave scientists who had followed her into battle despite their lack of training.

As she reflected on the battle, she realized that the Empire's attack was not just an act of aggression but a threat to the entire galaxy. She knew that the Terran Empire would stop at nothing to conquer and dominate every planet they came across and would not rest until they achieved their ultimate goal.

And the haunting of how the Empire knew of her arrival continued to hang in the air. Who and how were questions still to be answered.

The battle made Zara's determination to see the Empire defeated stronger than ever. She knew that the UIA needed to take action to prevent the Empire from further spreading its destruction. She vowed to use her skills and knowledge to develop new technologies and strategies to fight against the Empire, protect innocent lives, and prevent more tragedies like the one on Eurydice from happening again.

As she sat in the outpost's quiet, Zara promised her fallen team that their sacrifice would not be in vain. She would do everything in her power to ensure that the Empire would pay for their atrocities and that their reign of terror would come to an end.

Zara sat staring at the picture of the bunker on Eurydice on her computer screen. She couldn't get the memory of the slaughter out of her mind, but she was more determined than ever to get back to the planet and retrieve the information and technology she had seen in the bunker.

Zara was also driven by a deep desire for justice. The attack on her team had been unprovoked and ruthless. Zara was convinced that the only way to stop the Empire was to learn more about them and their tactics and to use that knowledge to mount a coordinated resistance.

But Zara also wondered what had happened to the inhabitants of Eurydice. The artifacts in the bunker had hinted at a once-thriving civilization that had been abruptly wiped out, and Zara was determined to learn more about who they were and what had led to their demise. She knew that the answers lay on Eurydice and was willing to do whatever it took to uncover them.

Despite the risks, Zara was resolute in her determination to return to Eurydice. She knew that the information and technology she could obtain there would be vital in the fight against the Empire and that the artifacts and documents she discovered would provide critical insight into the history and culture of the planet. Zara was determined to unlock Eurydice's secrets and use that knowledge to help defeat the Empire once and for all.

As the idea of returning to Eurydice began to crystallize in Zara's mind, she faced the formidable task of preparing her crew for the challenges ahead. The control room of the outpost on Aurora Beta buzzed with a sense of purpose as Zara assembled her team for a crucial briefing. Holographic displays illuminated the room, projecting images of

Eurydice's alien landscape and the remnants of the bunker, a silent testimony to their past struggles.

Zara's words resonated with determination as she outlined the mission's objectives and risks. The crew, a diverse assembly of explorers and specialists, absorbed the weight of the impending journey. The murmurs of uncertainty gave way to a collective nod of agreement as Zara emphasized the significance of what they aimed to achieve on Eurydice – unlocking the secrets that could turn the tide against the Terran Empire.

The crew's response was a testament to their unwavering trust in Zara's leadership. Fueled by a shared commitment to exploration and the pursuit of knowledge, each member expressed their readiness to face the unknown. Their collective dedication, a blend of excitement and trepidation, became the cornerstone upon which the mission's success would be built.

However, the journey back to Eurydice was not solely within the jurisdiction of Zara and her crew. The approval of the UIA commanders was imperative for such a risky and unprecedented mission. In a high-stakes meeting, Zara was to present her case before the UIA leadership, outlining the strategic importance of returning to Eurydice.

The meeting room within the UIA headquarters on Aurora Beta was a realm of tense deliberation as Zara faced the grueling challenge of convincing the commanders to approve the perilous mission back to Eurydice. The holographic displays flickered with images of the alien planet, casting an eerie glow over the assembled officials. The air hung heavy with anticipation, each breath echoing the gravity of the decision at hand.

Standing at the forefront, Zara carried the weight of her past experiences on Eurydice like a mantle of determination. Her eyes, lit with the fire of conviction, scanned the faces of the commanders. The questions of risk and potential consequences reverberated through the room, the unspoken concerns casting a shadow over the atmosphere.

With measured eloquence, Zara began weaving a narrative that drew from the fabric of her past struggles on Eurydice. She spoke of the sacrifices made by her previous crew, the echoes of their unwavering commitment haunting the edges of her words. The holographic displays shifted to images of the remnants of the bunker, a silent testament to the perils and potential rewards that awaited them.

In the hushed room, Zara painted a vivid picture of the potential benefits for humanity that lay hidden among the secrets of Eurydice. Her words resonated with a passion born of the belief that unlocking the mysteries of the alien planet could shift the balance in the ongoing cosmic struggle against the Terran Empire. The potential for advanced technology, intelligence, and cultural insights became a beacon of hope in the cosmic darkness.

As Zara spoke, the tension in the room became palpable. Commanders exchanged glances, furrowed brows, and contemplative expressions betraying the weight of their decisions. Conversations unfolded in whispers among the officials, debates on risk and reward rippling through the gathering. The potential consequences of the mission, both for Zara and the UIA, hung in the air like an unspoken challenge.

Zara, recognizing the weight of the moment, dove into a spirited dialogue with the commanders. Her approach was a delicate dance between reason and passion, a blend of strategic acumen and impassioned rhetoric. With a measured cadence, she began by methodically addressing each concern raised by the commanders.

Drawing on her experiences on Eurydice, Zara offered a nuanced analysis of the potential risks involved. She outlined detailed contingency plans, demonstrating a keen understanding of the intricacies of the mission. Her words were a reassurance and a strategic roadmap designed to mitigate uncertainties and pave the way for a successful exploration.

As the discussion unfolded, Zara's impassioned rhetoric took center stage. Her conviction shone through as she painted a vivid picture of the cosmic possibilities awaiting discovery on Eurydice. The potential benefits, she argued, extended beyond the realm of mere exploration. They encompassed advancements in technology, profound insights into the nature of the universe, and a cultural tapestry waiting to be unraveled.

Emphasizing the calculated nature of the mission, Zara stressed that the pursuit of knowledge and technological advancement was at the core of the UIA's mission. She reminded the commanders that the organization was founded on principles that embraced the unknown, propelled by a collective commitment to pushing the boundaries of cosmic understanding.

With a fervor that echoed through the dimly lit meeting room, Zara painted a vision of a future where the UIA stood at the forefront of cosmic enlightenment. She spoke of their responsibility, not just to themselves but to all of humanity. She argued that the potential discoveries on Eurydice had the power to shape the course of history and redefine the balance of power in the cosmic struggle against the Terran Empire.

Zara's words resonated in this exchange of ideas, creating a ripple effect through the room. The once tense atmosphere began to shift, as some commanders, initially skeptical, found themselves swayed by the combination of Zara's logical reasoning and passionate vision. The meeting room, once a crucible of uncertainty, now echoed with the renewed vigor of exploration and the pursuit of knowledge. Zara's spirited dialogue had become a catalyst for a collective decision that would carry profound consequences for the future of UIA's cosmic endeavors.

The meeting room became a crucible of emotions, the ebb and flow of arguments echoing the cosmic struggle they faced. Zara's determination to secure approval for the mission, guided by the lessons learned from Eurydice, became a rallying cry that resonated with the spirit of exploration that defined the UIA.

The dim glow of the holographic displays marked the conclusion of a heated debate within the UIA headquarters. As the collective decision ripened in the crucible of deliberations, the commanders reached a pivotal moment with furrowed brows and contemplative expressions.

The heart of the debate lay in a meticulous examination of the risks associated with returning to Eurydice. Commanders raised concerns about the unknown variables, the potential threats lurking within the alien planet's enigmatic confines. They deliberated on the lessons learned from the previous mission, dissecting the events that unfolded on Eurydice and assessing the implications for a second foray.

Arguments ebbed and flowed through the room like cosmic currents. Some commanders, cautious and pragmatic, emphasized the importance of minimizing risks to ensure the safety of exploration teams. Inspired by Zara's impassioned plea, others advocated for the profound benefits that awaited discovery on Eurydice, presenting a vision where the UIA could seize a pivotal moment in cosmic exploration.

The potential consequences of the mission loomed large, casting shadows over the deliberations. Each aspect was scrutinized, from the technological intricacies of the spacecraft to the psychological toll on the exploration team. The delicate balance between risk and reward became the fulcrum upon which the mission's fate rested.

Zara's strategic reasoning and impassioned rhetoric played a crucial role in swaying the tide of the debate. She addressed each concern with a meticulous approach, offering solutions and contingencies that spoke to the commanders' practical sensibilities. The calculated nature of the mission, with a focus on extracting valuable knowledge and technological insights, resonated with the UIA's core mission.

In the end, as the holographic displays dimmed, the commanders arrived at a collective decision. The approval for the perilous mission back to Eurydice was granted as a testament to the belief in the spirit of exploration and the pursuit of knowledge that defined the UIA. The decision represented a harmonious fusion of caution and curiosity, a nod to the organization's commitment to pushing the boundaries of cosmic understanding while navigating the uncharted territories of the unknown.

In the wake of the tense deliberations, the UIA commanders, while granting preliminary approval for Zara's mission to Eurydice, added a crucial condition before the final green light was given. They mandated a comprehensive study of the Terran Empire's fleets, their ideology, and battle strategies. The holographic displays within the meeting room flickered to life again, projecting intricate details of the imperial forces, their formidable armada, and the underlying tenets that fueled their expansionist ambitions.

Now tasked with a dual mission, Zara embraced the additional responsibility with a steely resolve. Studying the Terran Empire's strengths and weaknesses would become a cornerstone in formulating a strategic approach for the impending journey to Eurydice. Once saturated with tension, the room hummed with focused determination as Zara and the commanders delved into the nuances of the enemy they would confront on the cosmic frontier. The final green light hung in the balance, contingent upon Zara's ability to unravel the mysteries of Eurydice and the formidable adversary that lurked beyond the stars.

The outpost on Aurora Beta pulsed with vibrant energy as the crew diligently readied themselves for the impending journey back to Eurydice. Every corner echoed with the cadence of hurried footsteps, the metallic resonance a prelude to the cosmic odyssey that awaited them. The hum of spacecraft engines intertwined with the frenetic activity, creating a harmonious symphony of anticipation.

Engineers fine-tuned the spacecraft's intricate systems in the technical bays, ensuring that every component was calibrated to perfection. The metallic clang of tools against machinery punctuated the air as they meticulously inspected and repaired any potential vulnerabilities. The spacecraft, a vessel of exploration and discovery, stood as a testament to human ingenuity, a fusion of advanced technology, and the collective aspirations of the UIA.

In the strategic planning chambers, Zara engaged in detailed discussions with mission specialists.

Charts and holographic displays illuminated the room, mapping the trajectory and contingencies for the upcoming expedition. The crew's roles and responsibilities were outlined with military precision, each member aware of their crucial contribution to the mission's success.

Clad in specialized suits designed for cosmic exploration, the crew underwent final training sessions. The weightlessness simulator, a crucial element of their preparation, allowed them to acclimate to the conditions they would face in the cosmic vacuum. The camaraderie among the crew members served as a source of strength, a shared determination to face the unknown and emerge victorious.

As the spacecraft's cargo holds were stocked with provisions, supplies, and cutting-edge scientific equipment, the outpost became a bustling hub of activity. The research and exploration tools, meticulously calibrated for the unique challenges of Eurydice, were carefully stowed, awaiting deployment on the alien planet's surface.

The preparation extended beyond the technical aspects; it became a psychological and emotional readiness for the cosmic voyage. As the leader, Zara provided guidance and inspiration, fostering a sense of unity among the crew. Briefings on the potential challenges and the magnitude of their mission instilled a collective resolve, forging a bond that transcended the confines of the spacecraft.

The outpost on Aurora Beta, a temporal haven nestled on the cosmic fringes, witnessed the convergence of human determination and cosmic curiosity. With its intricate components and orchestrated movements, the symphony of preparation heralded the imminent departure. The return to Eurydice was not just a journey through space but a declaration of humanity's indomitable spirit in the face of the cosmic unknown.

The Terran Empire

The Terran Empire had been expanding its territory for decades, and tensions between them and the UIA had steadily risen. Zara had been assigned to Aurora Beta, a UIA outpost on the edge of Terran space, monitoring the Empire's movements and relaying information back to headquarters.

The Terran Empire, a formidable interstellar civilization, was led by a charismatic and astute leader, Emperor Maximus Decimus. Emperor Decimus wielded unparalleled influence over the vast expanse of the Empire, and his control over the government, military, and populace was absolute. His leadership style was characterized by strategic brilliance, political cunning, and an iron-fisted approach to maintaining order and dominance.

Emperor Decimus surrounded himself with a cadre of four key assistants, each playing a crucial role in the governance and expansion of the Terran Empire:

1. **General Valeria Drakonov:** As the Supreme Commander of the Terran military forces, General Drakonov was responsible for executing the emperor's military strategies. Known for her tactical genius and unyielding loyalty to Emperor Decimus, she played a pivotal role in conquering

and subjugating various planets. Under her command, the Terran military achieved unprecedented efficiency and discipline.

2. **Grand Vizier Octavia Synestra:** Grand Vizier Synestra served as Emperor Decimus's chief political advisor. Her diplomatic finesse and ability to manipulate the political landscape were instrumental in expanding the Empire's influence without resorting to direct military intervention. Synestra was skilled at navigating the intricate web of interstellar politics, ensuring that the Terran Empire remained a dominant force in both military and diplomatic spheres.

3. **Scientific Advancer Quintus Caelum:** Quintus Caelum was the head of the Imperial Science Directorate, overseeing technological advancements and scientific developments within the Empire. His role was crucial in maintaining the technological edge that allowed the Terran military to outmatch its adversaries. Caelum's innovations ranged from advanced weaponry to cutting-edge propulsion systems, ensuring the Empire stayed at the forefront of scientific progress.

4. **Shadow Mistress Seraphina Nocturna:** Seraphina Nocturna was the enigmatic head of the Imperial Intelligence Network, specializing in espionage, sabotage, and information warfare. Her covert operations played a significant role in destabilizing rival civilizations and ensuring the

loyalty of conquered territories. Nocturna's ability to manipulate information and control the narrative contributed to the Empire's reputation for invincibility.

In terms of military power, the Terran Empire boasted one of the most formidable forces in the known universe. Thanks to advanced technology, disciplined troops, and strategic brilliance, their military prowess was unrivaled. The Terran military's universal rankings consistently placed them at the top, with fleets of powerful warships, highly trained ground forces, and the ability to project force across vast distances. The mere presence of the Terran military was often enough to compel submission from less powerful civilizations, solidifying the Empire's dominance on the interstellar stage.

The fleet of the Terran Empire was a formidable force to be reckoned with. It consisted of hundreds of vessels of various sizes and types, each designed for a specific combat role. Here is a detailed description of some of the most prominent types of ships in the Terran Empire's fleet:

· Dreadnoughts: These massive ships were the backbone of the Terran fleet. They were heavily armored and armed with various weapons, including laser cannons, missile launchers, and plasma beams. Dreadnoughts were used to provide long-range fire support and were often at the center of large fleet engagements.

· Battlecruisers: These ships were more minor than dreadnoughts but were still heavily armed and armored. Battlecruisers were used to engage enemy ships at medium range, using their advanced targeting systems and powerful weapons to take down their opponents.

· Frigates: Frigates were smaller than battlecruisers but could still hold their own in combat. They were often used for reconnaissance and escort duties, supporting larger ships in the fleet.

· Corvettes: These small, fast ships were used for hit-and-run attacks and disrupting enemy formations. They were armed with powerful missiles and torpedoes. They were often used to target larger ships' engines and weapons systems.

· Carriers: Large ships designed to carry and launch fighter craft. They were heavily armored and armed, and their fighter craft were used to engage enemy ships and defend larger vessels in the fleet.

In addition to their ships, the Terran Empire's fleet was also equipped with a wide range of advanced weaponry, including energy shields, cloaking devices, and robust AI systems. Their ships were powered by advanced fusion reactors. They could travel at faster-than-light speeds, making them a formidable force in any engagement.

The Terran Empire's belief in dominance and control was deeply rooted in a philosophy that exalted their exceptionalism and viewed other civilizations as mere stepping stones on the path to galactic supremacy. At the core of their ideology lay a fervent conviction that they were the rightful rulers of the entire galaxy, and this belief was fortified by a potent blend of militarism, expansionism, and a sense of manifest destiny.

For the Terrans, their civilization was not just one among many but the apex of evolutionary progress. They considered themselves the pinnacle of intelligence and power, ordained by fate to subjugate and govern the lesser beings scattered across the cosmos. The notion of superiority was ingrained in the very fabric of their society and echoed in their political doctrines, educational systems, and cultural narratives.

To the Terran Empire, the expansion of their dominion was not an act of aggression but a cosmic imperative. They saw themselves as guardians of order and believed that uniting the galaxy under their rule could bring about a utopian era of stability and progress. In their fervor, they regarded the civilizations they encountered as primitives; their rulership deemed a benevolent obligation to lift the galaxy from chaos.

This belief system fueled their militaristic endeavors and justified their conquests to spread what they considered the "enlightened" values of the Terran way. The concept of manifest destiny was woven into the very fabric of their identity, with the conviction that the galaxy's fate was inexorably intertwined with their own ascent to supremacy.

The Terran Empire's worldview, shaped by notions of exceptionalism and destiny, created a formidable adversary for those who dared to resist their expansionist ambitions. As Zara delved into understanding this ideology, she confronted a military adversary and an entrenched belief system that fueled the relentless march of the Terran forces across the cosmic expanse.

The United Intergalactic Alliance, on the other hand, was a coalition of planets and civilizations that banded together for mutual protection and cooperation. They believed in a philosophy of equality and cooperation, valuing diversity and the unique perspectives of different cultures.

As news of the Terran Empire's aggressive attack on Zara, a prominent figure within the United Intergalactic Alliance (UIA), spread across the cosmos, the entire universe was on high alert. The incident intensified the already simmering tensions between the Terran Empire and the UIA, propelling the galaxy into a state of uncertainty and unease.

The conflict between the two interstellar powers had deep roots, grounded in their conflicting philosophies and territorial ambitions. The Terrans, driven by a desire for dominance, perceived the UIA as a direct threat to their supremacy. Their imperialistic tendencies fueled a determination to bring the UIA, a coalition of diverse civilizations united by a commitment to peace and cooperation, under their authoritarian rule.

On the other side of the cosmic divide, the UIA regarded the Terran Empire as a perilous aggressor, a force whose expansionist endeavors threatened the stability and autonomy of countless planetary systems. The attack on Zara on Eurydice served as a stark reminder of the Terrans' ruthless pursuit of control, solidifying the UIA's resolve to resist and protect the freedom of its member civilizations.

The complexity of the situation was compounded by the sheer military might and advanced technology wielded by the Terran Empire and the UIA. Their formidable fleets, cutting-edge weaponry, and highly trained forces elevated the stakes of any potential conflict to unprecedented levels. The galaxy braced itself for the possibility of devastation on an astronomical scale.

As diplomatic channels strained under the weight of accusations and counter-accusations, the tension escalated to a point where even the neutral systems and unaligned civilizations found themselves caught in the gravitational pull of this cosmic power struggle. The delicate balance of alliances and treaties within the UIA began to strain, with some members advocating for a more assertive stance against the Terran threat. In contrast, others sought diplomatic resolutions to avoid an all-out war.

Undeterred by the mounting universal apprehension, the Terran Empire continued to assert its dominance, justifying its actions as necessary for preserving order and progress. The UIA, in response, initiated a mobilization of its military forces, forming a united front against the encroaching imperial menace.

The galaxy, once a tapestry of cooperation and shared exploration, now found itself on the brink of conflict that could reshape the destinies of countless worlds. The cosmos held its breath as the clash between the Terran Empire and the UIA unfolded, with the outcome poised to leave an indelible mark on the annals of interstellar history.

Echoes of Destiny

Inside the well-lit strategic briefing room, Zara's commanders, a council of seasoned experts in various fields, deliberated the next steps for the mission. The star maps flickered to life, showcasing the cosmic expanse and the distant silhouette of Eurydice. The tension in the room was palpable as they assessed the latest data streams and reports.

· **Surge in Cosmic Activity:** Sensor readings from the galaxy's outer rim indicated an unprecedented surge in cosmic activity near Eurydice. Unexplained anomalies, fluctuations in gravitational fields, and sporadic bursts of energy permeated the region. The council, recognizing the potential significance of these phenomena, concluded that now was a crucial moment to reevaluate their understanding of Eurydice's enigmatic nature.

· **Mysterious Signal:** Amidst the bustling preparations, a mysterious signal was intercepted by the outpost's communication array. The signal, coded in an ancient language previously unidentified, emanated from the vicinity of Eurydice. Initial attempts at decryption hinted at a message encrypted in the fabric of the cosmic waves, further compelling the commanders to initiate the return to Eurydice sooner than planned.

· **The Unveiling of Zara's Craft:** The council, recognizing the urgency of the situation, unveiled Zara's assigned vehicle for the mission—a state-of-the-art exploratory spacecraft equipped with cutting-edge astrophysical instruments and advanced propulsion systems. The sleek vessel, "Stellar Voyager," was designed for deep-space exploration, capable of maneuvering through intricate cosmic environments.

· **The Fleet Configuration:** Alongside the Stellar Voyager, a fleet of specialized support ships was designated for the expedition. These included nimble reconnaissance probes for data collection, resource mining vessels for planetary surveys, and defensive frigates equipped with advanced weaponry. The fleet was a testament to the commanders' meticulous planning and strategic foresight, tailored to handle a myriad of challenges expected in the uncharted territories of Eurydice.

As the decision to return to Eurydice echoed through the outpost, the crew transitioned from preparations to embarkation, their anticipation fueled by the promise of discovery and the unknown. Little did they realize that a surprise within the enigmatic folds of Eurydice would test their mettle and redefine the parameters of their interstellar odyssey.

The launch of the Stellar Voyager was a momentous occasion, marked by a symphony of mechanical precision and human anticipation. The outpost on Aurora Beta, bathed in the artificial glow of floodlights, became a hive of activity as the spacecraft stood poised on the launchpad. The metallic echo of boots against the floor resonated through the corridors, a prelude to the cosmic odyssey that awaited Zara and her crew.

Anticipation hung in the air like a tangible force, an electric charge that animated the crew's movements. At the forefront of the launch preparations, Zara exuded a quiet confidence that mirrored the vastness of the cosmos they were about to explore. Her eyes, reflecting the myriad stars visible through the viewport, sparkled with excitement and determination.

The Stellar Voyager, its sleek hull gleaming in the artificial light, stood as a testament to human ingenuity and the insatiable desire to reach beyond the boundaries of the known. Its specialized design, equipped with cutting-edge astrophysical instruments and advanced propulsion systems, symbolized the culmination of meticulous planning and technological innovation.

Adorned in specialized suits, the crew moved with practiced efficiency, each member contributing to the final checks and preparations. Engineers made last-minute adjustments, ensuring every component was in optimal condition for the cosmic journey. The atmosphere was charged with an undeniable sense of purpose—a collective commitment to unveil the secrets hidden among the stars.

As the countdown commenced, the hum of spacecraft engines joined the chorus of anticipation. Standing at the command center, Zara observed the pulsating lights on the control console, each blinking a heartbeat echoing the universal rhythm of exploration. Now strapped into their designated positions, the crew members exchanged glances filled with excitement and resolve.

The launch itself was a spectacle—a controlled eruption of power that lifted the Stellar Voyager from the launchpad and into the cosmic expanse beyond. The gravitational pull released its hold, and the spacecraft ascended gracefully, leaving the confines of Aurora Beta and venturing into the limitless depths of space.

Weightlessness enveloped the crew inside the spacecraft as they transitioned from the pull of gravity to the gentle drift of microgravity. With its holographic displays and star maps, the command center became the epicenter of their cosmic odyssey. Sitting at the helm, Zara guided the ship with a steady hand, her eyes fixed on the celestial canvas unfolding before them.

The crew, now weightless but anchored by the gravitational pull of purpose, engaged in final system checks and synchronized their instruments with the rhythmic hum of the spacecraft. The journey had begun, and the anticipation that had hung in the air now transformed into a tangible sense of awe—an acknowledgment of the boundless possibilities that awaited them in the cosmic unknown.

As the Stellar Voyager sailed through the expanse, leaving the outpost on Aurora Beta behind, the crew felt the vibrancy of their shared adventure. The distant yet inviting stars seemed to beckon them toward a destiny written in the cosmic tapestry. This destiny would unfold with each passing moment of the cosmic odyssey ahead.

The journey to Eurydice began with a serene drift through the cosmic currents, the Stellar Voyager gliding gracefully through the vastness of space. The initial leg of the trip was marked by a sense of anticipation, with the crew engaged in routine tasks. Zara periodically checking the navigational charts, each moment a step closer to unlocking the secrets that lay dormant on Eurydice.

As the spacecraft approached the edge of known space, a subtle shift in the cosmic winds signaled the onset of a cosmic anomaly. Typically calibrated to perfection, the navigational systems on the Stellar Voyager began to register irregularities. At first, it was mere blips on the monitoring screens—innocuous fluctuations that betrayed the chaotic undercurrents of the impending tempest.

The initial encounter with the tempest was unanticipated and abrupt. The calm drift transformed into a chaotic dance as the ship encountered the first ripples of the cosmic tempest. The Stellar Voyager, designed for precision and control, suddenly found itself at the mercy of forces beyond its programming. The ship swerved violently, tossed like a fragile vessel on a tempestuous sea.

Alarms erupted throughout the spacecraft, their blaring wails echoing through the metallic corridors. The hull groaned under the pressure of the tempest's turbulent currents, and the hum of the engines was drowned by the howling winds of the celestial storm. The crew, caught off guard by the sudden onslaught, struggled to find footing as the ship lurched and trembled.

Zara, seated at the command center, reacted with a swift determination. Her eyes, wide with urgency, scanned the blinking panels of the control console. Warning lights painted the room in an eerie glow as the ship's systems registered the onslaught of cosmic forces. Zara's fingers danced across the holographic interface, attempting to stabilize the vessel and plot a course through the tempest.

The initial danger was palpable—a ship caught in the tempest's grasp, its systems strained to their limits. The crew, thrown into disarray, responded with panic and urgency. Voices clamored over the ship's intercom as each crew member grappled with their respective stations, attempting to mitigate the effects of the tempest on the vessel's delicate balance.

The initial danger was palpable; it was an existential threat gripping the Stellar Voyager in a vice of cosmic fury. The tempest's forces strained the ship to the very brink of disaster. The hull creaked and groaned under the onslaught of tumultuous energy. The delicate balance of the spacecraft's intricate systems teetered on the edge of collapse.

In those critical moments, the crew was on the precipice of chaos. Panic and urgency rippled through the ship like a shockwave. Each crew member, trained to face the unknown with unwavering resolve, now grappled with the harsh reality of the cosmic tempest. Stations flickered with warning lights, and alarms echoed through the metallic corridors, amplifying the sense of impending doom.

Laden with stress and urgency, Voices clamored over the ship's intercom, creating a dissonant cacophony of fear and determination. The chaos was palpable in the command center, where Zara stood at the helm. The holographic star maps, designed to provide clarity, flickered and danced in erratic patterns, mirroring the tempest's chaotic energy. The very heart of the ship's control, once a bastion of order, now reflected the turbulence that gripped the vessel.

Amidst the pandemonium, Zara's voice emerged as a beacon of stability. Steady and authoritative, she cut through the tumult like a lighthouse piercing the stormy night. Her commands, issued with precision, defied the logical constraints that typically governed spacecraft maneuvers. Emergency protocols, usually reserved for extreme circumstances, were activated in a desperate bid to regain control.

"Engage reverse thrusters! Full power to the stabilizers! Brace for impact!" Zara's orders, though counterintuitive, were a testament to her astrophysical intuition and leadership under pressure. The crew, their faith anchored in Zara's guidance, executed maneuvers that defied the laws of conventional space navigation.

The Stellar Voyager, battered and tossed like a leaf in a tempest, responded to the crew's collective efforts. Reverse thrusters hummed with newfound vigor, stabilizers strained against the cosmic onslaught, and the ship's initially chaotic and unpredictable trajectory began to align with a semblance of order.

Despite the chaos, Zara's voice, steady and authoritative, cut through the tumult. She issued orders with precision, directing the crew to engage in emergency protocols and reinforcing the importance of unity in the face of imminent danger. The Stellar Voyager, battered and tossed by the cosmic forces, became a microcosm of resilience as the crew, guided by Zara's unwavering leadership, worked in unison to navigate the storm and keep their vessel intact.

Inside the command center, the crew worked with synchronized determination. Displays flickered, fingers danced across holographic interfaces, and the air hummed with a fusion of stress and concentration. Her resolute in her commitment to navigate the ship through the storm, Zara maintained a vigil over the chaos, her eyes fixed on the swirling patterns of the tempest outside.

The dance through the cosmic chaos tested skill, determination, and shared will. Against all odds, the crew, guided by Zara's unwavering leadership, wrestled the Stellar Voyager from the clutches of imminent disaster. Though battered and bruised, the ship emerged on the other side of the tempest—a symbol of resilience in the face of cosmic perils.

As the Stellar Voyager sailed through the calmer cosmic currents beyond the tempest, a subdued tension lingered among the crew. Still seated at the command center, Zara couldn't shake the unease that settled within her. The tempest, a celestial surprise, raised questions that echoed through the confines of the spacecraft.

"Why wasn't the tempest detected earlier?" Zara mused aloud, her voice carrying a note of contemplation. The crew exchanged puzzled glances, grappling with the mystery that had engulfed them.

Zara's mind turned to the possibility of an unseen enemy, a force capable of orchestrating the cosmic tempest with intent. The idea of an adversary shrouded in the enigmatic depths of space sparked a sense of urgency within her. Was the tempest a natural phenomenon, or had it been artificially created by a faction with advanced technology previously unknown to them?

The unsettling thought lingered, prompting Zara to consider the involvement of the Terran Empire. Could this tempest be a covert weapon, manifesting their insidious influence in the cosmic theater? The idea of the Terran Empire possessing technology capable of manipulating cosmic forces sent shivers through Zara's spine.

Determined to unravel the mystery, Zara engaged the crew in a comprehensive analysis of the tempest's effects on the ship's systems. As they delved into the data, each piece of information became a puzzle piece in a larger, more ominous picture. The Stellar Voyager, now sailing through the aftermath of the cosmic tempest, carried the scars of the encounter and the weight of unanswered questions that would shape the trajectory of their cosmic odyssey.

Resurgence of the Past

After the harrowing dance with the cosmic tempest, the Stellar Voyager sailed through the cosmic currents with an eerie calmness. The hum of the spacecraft's engines was a steady lullaby, starkly contrasting the previous tumult. Inside the vessel, the crew, still recovering from the tempest's onslaught, moved with cautious optimism. The holographic star maps displayed serene constellations, and tranquility permeated the ship's corridors.

Sitting at the command center, Zara observed the calm with a mixture of relief and suspicion. The eeriness of the stillness hung in the air, and she couldn't shake the feeling that this apparent calmness might be the precursor to another cosmic storm. The crew, too, exchanged glances that mirrored a shared wariness—an unspoken acknowledgment that the cosmic unknown was a fickle companion.

As the spacecraft traversed the cosmic expanse en-route to Eurydice, the quietude became a canvas of anticipation. Zara, driven by an insatiable curiosity, contemplated the mysteries that awaited them on the enigmatic planet. The passage felt like the calm before the storm, a deceptive serenity that heightened her senses and steeled her resolve for whatever lay ahead.

The descent onto Eurydice was a slow, deliberate ballet of cosmic proportions. The planet, a distant orb shrouded in mist, grew larger on the viewscreens, and the crew's attention shifted from the celestial calm to the imminent rendezvous with their destination. Eurydice, a world steeped in the unknown, beckoned with the promise of discoveries yet unveiled.

Standing at the command center, Zara felt a peculiar blend of excitement and caution. The tranquility of the passage had done little to dispel the lingering doubts in the corners of her mind. Was this eerily calm journey leading them into the embrace of an unseen adversary, a trap carefully laid in the cosmic void? The prospect of the Terran Empire's influence, shrouded in the enigma of space, lingered like a shadow over her thoughts.

The crew braced for the unknown as the Stellar Voyager descended through the planet's atmosphere. The descent was almost too smooth, creating an uneasy tension that wrapped itself around the spacecraft. The holographic displays painted a serene picture of Eurydice's surface, but the crew's vigilance remained unwavering.

The landing was a gentle embrace, the spacecraft touching Eurydice's surface with a soft thud. The metallic hull settled against the unknown terrain, silencing the spacecraft's engines. The airlocks hissed open, and the crew, clad in exploration suits, stepped onto the surface of Eurydice.

Zara, the first to set foot on the alien soil, felt a surge of anticipation. The eeriness of the calm passage persisted, casting a surreal glow over the landscape. The crew dispersed, deploying scientific instruments and setting up a temporary base camp. Despite the apparent calm, Zara couldn't shake the sense of being watched. This nagging intuition whispered warnings of potential danger.

Zara led the way as the crew ventured into the mysterious landscape, her eyes scanning the horizon. The stillness of Eurydice contrasted with the cosmic turbulence they had faced earlier, and the uncanny calmness heightened the crew's sense of vulnerability. Every footstep echoed with a weight of anticipation—a delicate dance between the serenity of the unknown and the potential for cosmic turmoil.

The enigma of Eurydice awaited, and with a mixture of caution and determination, Zara led her crew into the uncharted depths of the alien world, ready to unveil the secrets hidden beneath its tranquil facade.

Eurydice's air was thick with anticipation as Zara, accompanied by a small team, made her way towards the familiar rocky outcrop concealing the entrance to the abandoned bunker. The journey was a nostalgic echo, a return to a refuge that had shielded her from the storm of the Terran Empire's assault.

The bunker's entrance, weathered and worn, welcomed them with a creak as Zara pushed open the door. The dim light within flickered to life, revealing the same spacious chamber that had provided sanctuary during the previous encounter. However, this time, Zara's focus was not on evasion but exploration.

As she moved deeper into the bunker, Zara's gaze caught subtle details she had missed in the hurried escape. The metallic walls seemed to hum with ancient energy, and faint symbols etched into the surfaces hinted at a purpose beyond mere shelter.

Guided by a memory that had etched the bunker's layout into her mind, Zara approached a section of the wall that had always intrigued her. With a careful sweep of her hand, she explored its surface, searching for irregularities or hidden seams. A quiet gasp escaped her as she detected a subtle vibration beneath her touch.

Her instincts guided her. Zara pressed against the concealed mechanism, and with a hiss, a portion of the wall slid aside, revealing a passage that led deeper into the heart of the bunker. The team exchanged glances, their anticipation matching

Zara's, as they ventured into the newfound chambers.

The air grew cooler as they descended through a corridor adorned with symbols and markings that seemed to tell a story lost to time. Zara, her eyes gleaming with a mix of excitement and curiosity, led the way, her steps echoing through the metallic labyrinth.

The hidden chambers unveiled themselves like chapters in ancient times. Rooms filled with unknown technology lay dormant, waiting for someone to decipher their mysteries. Zara's team marveled at the advanced machinery; its purpose obscured by the veil of ages.

Zara and her team discovered a holographic console in one of the chambers surrounded by celestial diagrams and star maps. As she approached, the holographic display flickered to life, revealing intricate details of cosmic configurations that extended far beyond the knowledge of the UIA.

The star maps were not just astronomical charts; they were a cosmic tapestry weaving together constellations, galaxies, and celestial phenomena in a way that defied conventional understanding. Her eyes traced the patterns of unknown galaxies and celestial bodies. Zara felt a strange resonance with the information displayed.

It wasn't just the unprecedented detail that captivated her but a sensation that stirred a distant memory. As if the cosmic dance before her eyes was a reawakening of something buried deep within her consciousness. The intricate details seemed strangely familiar, like a half-remembered dream from her childhood.

Zara's mind flashed back to her younger years spent with Thalia, her childhood friend who had joined her as they traversed through the realms of the unknown. A sensation of déjà vu tingled in the recesses of her mind, hinting at a connection between her past and the celestial patterns unfolding in the holographic display.

She couldn't shake the feeling that, as a child, she had witnessed these cosmic configurations in some form. Perhaps it was during those nights when Thalia, with an enigmatic smile, pointed to the stars and whispered tales of ancient mysteries. The star maps felt like a bridge between her past and present, a connection that transcended the boundaries of time.

As Zara became captivated by the unfolding cosmic revelations, a persistent thought nagged at the edges of her consciousness. She couldn't shake the wondering about the source of this celestial knowledge. How had these star maps managed to elude the UIA's grasp? What arcane secrets of the universe were intricately woven into this cosmic tapestry that now called out to her for further exploration?

The enigma of the star maps carried a weighty implication. Zara found herself contemplating whether this intricate knowledge was precisely what the Terran Empire had sought to obtain or prevent her from discovering before they could. The very existence of this hidden chamber, filled with celestial insights beyond the UIA's reach, hinted at a cosmic puzzle that might hold the key to uncharted realms – a puzzle that the Terran Empire might have been desperate to solve or suppress. The connection between the Terran Empire's interference and the celestial revelations before her fueled Zara's determination to uncover the depths of this mysterious cosmic knowledge.

The holographic display became a portal to uncharted realms. Zara, guided by an inexplicable connection, delved into the depths of the star maps, her journey unfolding as a cosmic odyssey with echoes of the past whispering through the cosmic winds.

As Zara and her intrepid crew ventured deeper into the recesses of the bunker, the atmosphere grew charged with anticipation. The air seemed to crackle with a sense of discovery, and Zara's steps quickened as if propelled by an invisible force. In the heart of the bunker, a concealed chamber revealed itself. Zara's eyes widened with recognition — a trove of intricate devices, reminiscent of the mysterious technology she had glimpsed during her initial escape from the Terran Empire.

The devices, arranged in a mesmerizing array, hummed with latent power, casting a soft glow that danced across the chamber's metallic surfaces. Zara's scientific curiosity ignited like a supernova, and her mind raced with possibilities. Each device seemed a relic from a technologically advanced civilization that had left enigmatic remnants on Eurydice.

The first device she approached was an intricately designed console with holographic displays that seemed to shift and morph, responding to her presence. As Zara reached out to interact with the holograms, she felt a peculiar connection, an intuitive understanding of the alien interface. It was as if the technology recognized her, responding to a latent connection transcending time and space boundaries.

Adjacent to the holographic console, Zara's gaze fell upon a cluster of crystalline structures, each emitting a soft, pulsating light. As she approached, the crystals seemed to resonate in harmony with the energy coursing through the chamber. The rhythmic pulsations hinted at an underlying cosmic order, a language of energy that beckoned Zara to decipher its cosmic symphony.

Further exploration revealed a series of cylindrical pods suspended in a weightless state. Encased in a shimmering energy field, the pods exuded an otherworldly allure. Zara speculated on their purpose, considering the possibility of advanced stasis or preservation technology. What stories lay within these ethereal capsules, and who were the beings that once occupied them?

The chamber expanded into a vast knowledge repository, and Zara marveled at the complexity of the devices around her. She discovered a crystalline, suspended mid-air matrix that seemed to hold information within its luminescent core. As she interfaced with the matrix, a flood of data surged into her consciousness — star maps, celestial configurations, and cosmic phenomena previously unknown to the UIA.

As Zara interfaced with the crystalline matrix, the transition from the familiar to the extraordinary was seamless. Yet, the experience was nothing short of transcendental. The luminescent core pulsed with a radiant energy that seemed to resonate with the essence of the cosmos. As she touched the matrix, Zara felt an immediate connection. This ethereal bridge transported her consciousness beyond the confines of time and space.

A torrent of data surged into her mind, overwhelming in its scope and intricacy. Star maps materialized before her, intricate celestial configurations unfurled like cosmic tapestries, and the fabric of space-time seemed to ripple with the echoes of the universe's beginnings. Zara was no longer confined to the limitations of her physical self; she had become a voyager through the corridors of existence, witnessing the dance of galaxies and the birth of stars.

The luminescent matrix was a conduit to the ancient whispers of the universe, revealing cosmic phenomena previously concealed from the prying eyes of the UIA. Zara immersed herself in the mysteries of celestial bodies, their interconnected dance narrating the story of creation itself. The star maps, alive with the pulse of cosmic energies, unveiled constellations that defied the boundaries of known space as if charting a course through the very essence of creation.

Amid the torrent of cosmic revelations, a peculiar sense of recognition washed over Zara, as if the celestial wonders unfolding before her were not entirely unfamiliar. The connection resonated through the labyrinth of her memories, beckoning her back to the days spent with Thalia, a childhood friend who had served as both a warning and a mysterious guide. This resonance surpassed the limitations of conventional knowledge; it was an intrinsic link etched into the very essence of her existence.

As Zara navigated the cosmic data pulsating through the crystalline matrix, a subtle awareness whispered to her senses. In the vastness of the cosmic tapestry, she felt the presence of a familiar face observing her, a phantom of recognition that danced at the edges of her perception. Striving for clarity, Zara focused her gaze on the cosmic currents and, in a fleeting moment, glimpsed what seemed to be Thalia watching her.

The visage of Thalia, though brief, appeared as a flicker within the cosmic expanse. Her eyes, radiant with otherworldly wisdom, met Zara's in a transient connection that transcended the boundaries of time and space. It was not the mentor and guide from Zara's memories, but a haunting specter of a childhood companion moved by enigmatic forces.

The resonance persisted, intertwining Zara's consciousness with the cosmic dance around her. The connection to Thalia, now veiled in cosmic mysteries, added a layer of complexity to the revelations unfolding in the chamber. Zara stood at the crossroads of her memories and the cosmic wonders, a voyager entwined with the echoes of her past and the enigmatic forces that guided her through the cosmic currents.

Zara felt a profound sense of awe and humility in this moment of revelation. The data's enormity overwhelmed her, yet she embraced the cosmic symphony that enveloped her consciousness. She witnessed galaxies colliding in a celestial ballet, supernovae unleashing their cosmic fury, and the birth of planets cradled by the gentle hands of gravity.

The crystalline matrix became a gateway to the universe's timeline, a tapestry woven with threads of cosmic evolution. Zara stood at the nexus of creation, witnessing the unfolding drama of the cosmos. It was as if she had transcended the boundaries of her mortal self, becoming a celestial observer in the grand theater of existence.

The luminescent core pulsated with information that transcended the limits of human comprehension. Zara's mind grappled with the vastness of the data like a lone star navigating the cosmic expanse. She saw not only the beginnings of the universe but also glimpses of its distant future, a celestial journey that unfolded before her in a kaleidoscope of celestial hues.

As the flood of data continued, Zara became a vessel of cosmic awareness, a conduit through which the universe spoke. The crystalline matrix, suspended in the heart of the chamber, held the keys to a celestial library, and Zara was the seeker, unraveling the mysteries inscribed in the luminous core.

Overwhelmed yet exhilarated, Zara marveled at the interconnectedness of the cosmos. The crystalline matrix, a beacon of cosmic knowledge, had transported her beyond the realm of ordinary understanding. She stood on the precipice of the unknown, a witness to the symphony of the stars. In that moment, the universe unfolded its secrets to her eager mind.

Each device uncovered in the chamber hinted at a civilization that had harnessed the fabric of the cosmos for both knowledge and power. Zara's initial glimpses during her escape now unfolded into a cosmic tapestry, weaving together threads of advanced science, ancient wisdom, and a connection that transcended the boundaries of mere technology.

In the heart of this technological archive, Zara stood at the intersection of the known and the unknown, a bridge between the distant past and an uncertain future. The secrets dormant within these devices beckoned to be unraveled, promising insights that could reshape the very understanding of the universe itself. As she delved deeper into the mysteries of the chamber, Zara couldn't help but wonder — what cosmic truths awaited her discovery, and how would this newfound knowledge reshape the course of their expedition on Eurydice?

The pinnacle of revelation manifested when Zara ventured into a chamber aglow with an ethereal luminescence. At its epicenter stood an ancient console, its controls intricately adorned with symbols that mirrored the enigmatic markings on the bunker walls. As Zara approached, a resonant energy filled the air, causing the console to awaken, projecting a holographic interface that seemed to acknowledge her presence.

The holographic display unfurled a visual symphony of cosmic wonders, revealing celestial phenomena that transcended the grasp of ordinary comprehension. The symbols on the console danced with ethereal grace, their intricate patterns conveying a language older than the universe itself. As Zara navigated the interface, each touch resonated with a cosmic harmony, unraveling layers of knowledge deeply embedded within Eurydice.

The symbols, cryptic and arcane, pulsed with their own life, inviting the team to decipher the mysteries concealed within. However, as they endeavored to document the symbols, an uncanny phenomenon unfolded – the symbols dissipated like ephemeral mist, leaving a sense of bewilderment and an augmented veil of mystery.

Driven by scientific curiosity, Zara's team sought to capture the elusive symbols through advanced recording devices and holographic imaging. Yet, the symbols defied attempts at documentation, slipping away as if cosmic knowledge resisted containment within the conventional confines of technology.

The holographic display showcased the celestial wonders and provided glimpses into the primordial moments of the universe's birth. Swirling nebulas, cascading stellar formations, and cosmic energies intertwining in a celestial dance unfolded before their eyes. However, the magnitude of these revelations exceeded the grasp of human comprehension, leaving Zara and her team in awe of the vast cosmic tapestry that extended beyond the boundaries of their understanding.

The technology embedded within Eurydice's heart became a bridge to the ineffable, a portal through which the team glimpsed the enigmatic origins of the cosmos. The ancient console served as a conduit to an arcane knowledge that seemed to transcend time itself, offering fragments of the cosmic narrative that unfolded since the dawn of existence. Each interaction with the holographic interface became a delicate dance with the mysteries of the universe, a symphony of discovery that echoed through the chambers of the bunker, leaving Zara and her team humbled by the infinite complexity of the cosmos.

As they delved deeper, Zara couldn't help but wonder about the connection between the bunker's unknown technology and the distress signal from the Terran Empire. Was there a correlation, a cosmic web entwining their mission, with the enigmatic forces that lingered on Eurydice?

Once a refuge, the bunker had transformed into a gateway to the cosmos. Standing at the intersection of past and present, Zara felt the weight of a responsibility that transcended the Terran Empire's territorial claims. The hidden chambers held the key to knowledge that could reshape humanity's understanding of the universe.

With newfound revelations and unanswered questions, Zara and her team continued to explore the depths of the bunker, their journey into the unknown unveiling the cosmic secrets that lay dormant within the heart of Eurydice.

Amidst the captivating revelations within the bunker, Zara felt a growing responsibility to share the cosmic mysteries uncovered with the UIA. The symbols, holographic displays, and glimpses into the universe's infancy presented a tapestry of knowledge beyond her understanding. It was time to return to the Voyager and relay these unprecedented findings.

Gathering her team within the heart of the bunker, Zara initiated a holographic communication link with the UIA command center. The shimmering projection of the UIA emblem appeared before them, and a familiar face materialized—the head of the command center, Dr. Evelyn Simmons.

"Zara, report your findings," Dr. Simmons requested her expression a mix of anticipation and urgency.

Taking a deep breath, Zara began to narrate the remarkable discoveries within the hidden chambers of Eurydice. She described the symbols, the holographic displays, and the enigmatic technology that seemed to hold the secrets of the cosmos. However, she stressed the limitation of her understanding, acknowledging that the revelations surpassed the grasp of current human knowledge.

Dr. Simmons listened intently, her eyes widening as Zara unfolded the extraordinary narrative. The implications of the newfound knowledge were profound, and Zara sensed a shared awe in Dr. Simmons' reactions. The holographic projection flickered as she received the transmitted data from the bunker, capturing snippets of the cosmic wonders.

After a moment of silence, Dr. Simmons spoke, her voice resonating with a sense of gravity. "Zara, what you've discovered is beyond anything we could have imagined. The UIA will need to mobilize a fleet of specialists, scientists, and explorers to unravel the mysteries of Eurydice further. We need to understand the full extent of this cosmic knowledge."

Zara nodded in agreement, acknowledging the magnitude of the task at hand. "Dr. Simmons, I believe we've only scratched the surface. The technology here is ancient and holds information that could redefine our understanding of the universe. I recommend sending a team of experts capable of deciphering these symbols and comprehending the cosmic phenomena we've witnessed."

Dr. Simmons agreed, "We'll assemble a team of the brightest minds and specialists. Eurydice has become the focal point of an unprecedented scientific endeavor. The UIA will establish a colony with the necessary resources to sustain long-term exploration and research."

As the holographic link closed, Zara and her team prepared to return to the Voyager. The prospect of a UIA fleet descending upon Eurydice filled the air with a renewed sense of purpose. The journey back to the ship echoed with discussions about the future, the excitement of scientific collaboration, and the responsibility of humanity to unlock the cosmic mysteries that lay dormant on the barren surface of Eurydice.

The Voyager's engines roared to life as they lifted off Eurydice, leaving behind the mysterious bunker that harbored ancient knowledge. Zara gazed at the planet below, knowing that her discoveries would reshape the course of human exploration. The UIA, equipped with newfound revelations, would soon embark on a journey that transcended the boundaries of known space—a journey into the cosmic unknown.

A network of advanced surveillance technologies hummed with activity in the shadowy depths of the Terran Empire's clandestine chambers. Unbeknownst to Zara and her intrepid crew, every step within the ancient bunker on Eurydice was meticulously observed by the calculating eyes of the Empire. The holographic displays, symbols, and cosmic revelations were mirrored on their surveillance screens, granting the Empire an illicit glimpse into the cosmic secrets that unfolded within the hidden chambers.

Shadows of Dominion: The Dark Pact Unveiled

As Zara transmitted her findings to the UIA command center, the covert operatives of the Terran Empire, orchestrated by the cunning General Valeria Drakonov, moved swiftly to intercept the data. The interception unfolded seamlessly in the shadowy depths of the Imperial Intelligence Network, overseen by the enigmatic Shadow Mistress Seraphina Nocturna.

Unknown to Zara and her team, the Terran Empire, led by Supreme Commander Drakonov, possessed advanced technology that allowed them to covertly breach communication channels. Grand Vizier Synestra, the chief political advisor to General Drakonov, oversaw the strategic aspects of the operation, ensuring that every move aligned with the Empire's overarching goals.

The Imperial Science Directorate, led by Quintus Caelum, played a crucial role in decrypting and analyzing the transmitted data. Caelum's expertise ensured that the Terran Empire stayed one step ahead in understanding the cosmic revelations pouring in from Eurydice's ancient bunker.

As the UIA command center continued its transmission, the Terran Empire's operatives harnessed their newfound knowledge to discern the UIA's intent. Shadow Mistress Seraphina

Nocturna, known for her skill in subterfuge and manipulation, carefully assessed the implications of the information transmitted by Zara.

In the dimly lit chambers of the Imperial Intelligence Network, General Valeria Drakonov watched with a calculating gaze. The prospect of the UIA establishing a foothold on Eurydice fueled her determination to act swiftly. The clandestine interception marked the beginning of a covert race to Eurydice's secrets. This race could tip the balance of universal dominance in favor of the Terran Empire.

As the intercepted data unfolded, the Terran Empire's leaders convened to strategize their next move. Supreme Commander Drakonov, recognizing the strategic importance of Eurydice's revelations, knew that time was of the essence. With her mastery of intelligence and espionage, the enigmatic Shadow Mistress Seraphina Nocturna whispered insights that fueled the Empire's ambition.

In the heart of the Imperial Science Directorate, Quintus Caelum delved into cosmic data, extracting information that could give the Terran Empire a decisive advantage. Grand Vizier Synestra, the political architect, wove a narrative that would justify and galvanize the Empire's pursuit of Eurydice.

As the meeting concluded, General Valeria Drakonov's eyes, gleaming with ambition, knew exactly who to call upon to lead the Terran Empire in the race to Eurydice. The stage was set for a shadowed contest that would unfold in the cosmic tapestry of the universe.

The General leaned forward, keying a secure communication channel. "Initiate contact with Agent Xerion," the General's voice echoed through the dimly lit chamber. "We have a mission that requires finesse and ruthlessness. The fate of the Terran Empire hinges on securing the cosmic knowledge of Eurydice before the UIA." The dark silhouette of Agent Xerion, a shadowy operative known for ruthless efficiency, appeared on the holographic screen.

Agent Xerion, a cryptic figure veiled in shadows and whispered about in the clandestine corridors of power, emerged as an enigma within the cosmic tapestry of intrigue. The holographic screen flickered to life, casting an eerie glow that outlined the dark silhouette of this elusive operative, whose reputation for ruthless efficiency echoed through the annals of covert operations.

Little was known about Agent Xerion, and that lack of information contributed to the mystery that shrouded their identity. Like cosmic winds, rumors circulated among intelligence circles, weaving tales of unparalleled skill, an unwavering commitment to the Terran Empire, and a shadowy presence that left no room for error.

The origins of Agent Xerion were obscured in the cosmic mists, buried beneath layers of secrecy and obscured by the very nature of their clandestine profession. Some whispered that Xerion was a product of shadowy experiments, an embodiment of enhanced abilities honed to execute the Empire's darkest missions. Others speculated that the operative was a master of disguise, seamlessly blending into the cosmic backdrop, leaving no trace of their true identity.

The holographic representation captured the essence of Xerion's aura — a figure draped in an enigmatic cloak, face obscured by the shadows, and a presence that sent ripples of trepidation through even the most seasoned observers. The mention of Xerion's name invoked a sense of foreboding, a recognition that the Empire possessed an agent whose methods transcended the conventional boundaries of espionage.

The screen, now dominated by Xerion's presence, became a portal into the unknown, a glimpse into the world of covert maneuvers and strategic machinations. The operative's reputation for efficiency hinted at a record of successful missions, each executed with surgical precision and leaving no room for error.

As the holographic image lingered, the questions surrounding Agent Xerion deepened. What drove this shadowy figure? What allegiance or motivations guided their actions? The mystery of Xerion added another layer to the cosmic drama. This subplot unfolded in the shadows, away from the prying eyes of those who sought to unravel the enigma.

Agent Xerion's appearance on the holographic screen became a harbinger of uncertainty, a signal that the cosmic stage was set for a clandestine dance between shadows and light. The dark silhouette, a symbol of elusive prowess, left those who beheld it with a lingering sense of curiosity and trepidation as the cosmic chessboard awaited the next move in this intricate game of power and secrets.

The ominous alliance between the Terran Empire and their covert enforcer heralded an impending conflict that would unfold on the cosmic stage of Eurydice, where the fate of the universe hung in the balance.

In the UIA command center, the transmission was sent with hopeful anticipation, unaware that their cosmic revelations were already falling into the hands of those who thrived in the clandestine dance of universal dominance. The ever-watchful and calculating Terran Empire now possessed the key to the knowledge that could alter the cosmic balance of power.

Unbeknownst to Zara and her team, the dark interplay of forces had set in motion a race against time and an impending clash of civilizations, all obscured by the cosmic tapestry of Eurydice. The knowledge concealed within the bunker held the potential to tip the scales of universal dominance, a prize coveted by the Terran Empire for eons.

Echoes of Connection

The UIA headquarters reverberated with a symphony of activity. This cosmic cadence underscored the fervor of preparation for the imminent expedition to Eurydice. At the epicenter of this bustling cosmic dance, Zara was immersed in a whirlwind of responsibilities and tasks. The allure of the cosmic revelations, which had first beckoned her to Eurydice, still held her captive, infusing each decision with anticipation and scientific curiosity.

Zara's days were a meticulously choreographed series of events, a cosmic ballet of planning and coordination. Adorned with star charts and holographic displays, her office became a command center where she orchestrated the multifaceted preparations. Meetings with engineers, scientists, and strategists filled her schedule as she delved into the intricacies of spacecraft logistics, technological assessments, and security protocols.

Simultaneously, Zara navigated diplomatic discussions with UIA representatives, ensuring that the expedition adhered to interstellar regulations and ethical considerations. The delicate balance between scientific exploration and responsible governance required her deft touch. Zara embraced the challenge with the same fervor that fueled her passion for discovery.

The logistical preparations extended beyond Zara's office. The UIA headquarters buzzed with activity as engineers fine-tuned spacecraft engines, technicians calibrated advanced instruments, and a cadre of experts meticulously reviewed the mission's objectives. The fleet, an armada of cosmic explorers, underwent thorough inspections, ensuring that each vessel was equipped to withstand the enigmatic challenges of Eurydice.

Amidst the cosmic preparations, Zara engaged in briefings with her crew. Their diverse expertise, ranging from astrobiology to astrophysics, added layers of depth to the mission. Zara fostered an atmosphere of collaboration and shared purpose, emphasizing the significance of their quest to unravel the mysteries hidden within the cosmic enigma of Eurydice.

As she delved into the details of the mission plan, Zara navigated the cosmic unknown and the interpersonal dynamics within her team. Ensuring cohesion and unity among the diverse talents under her command became a parallel challenge that required the same leadership skills that had guided her through the shadows of Eurydice in the past.

Unbeknownst to Zara, the ghost from her past, Thalia moved within the corridors of the UIA headquarters. The intricate dance of preparation unfolded, oblivious to the undercurrents of manipulation that would shape the course of their cosmic journey.

Zara's office, a celestial tapestry of star charts and holographic displays, became the stage for an unexpected reunion. As Thalia stepped in, a momentary pause lingered on Zara's face before recognition dawned. "Thalia? Can it be you?"

Thalia, her smile concealing a well-veiled purpose, embraced Zara. "Zara, my friend, it's been too long." The hug carried the weight of untold stories, an unspoken history that time hadn't erased.

Zara, still grappling with the shock of the reunion, couldn't shake the memory of the holographic glimpse of Thalia in the bunker on Eurydice. "Thalia, I saw you in the bunker. A hologram, as if you were watching me. But I assumed..."

Thalia's eyes gleamed with genuine warmth. "Eurydice has a way of echoing our past, doesn't it? I've followed your progress, Zara. Your discoveries are truly remarkable."

Their conversation flowed seamlessly, guided by Thalia's adept touch. Skillfully steering the discussion toward the impending journey to Eurydice, Zara became a wellspring of information, unwittingly sharing details that held strategic value for the Terran Empire.

With a carefully concealed intent, Thalia probed into the specifics of the fleet's composition, extracting insights into the array of spacecraft at their disposal. Passionate about the cosmic odyssey ahead, Zara detailed the advanced propulsion systems, cutting-edge shielding technologies, and the collaborative efforts that had birthed these cosmic vessels.

As Zara spoke, she unraveled the intricate threads of the mission's security measures. The deployment of AI-driven sentinel probes, the encryption protocols safeguarding their communication channels, and the adaptive camouflage mechanisms designed to evade potential threats were all laid bare in the tapestry of her narrative.

The nuances of their exploration strategy became another unwitting offering. With genuine enthusiasm, Zara shared the intricacies of their approach to Eurydice, detailing how they intended to survey the surface, pinpoint potential sites of interest, and navigate the challenges posed by the alien planet's unique topography.

The cosmic dance between Zara and Thalia continued, each exchange a subtle tug at the strings of information that would weave through the impending expedition. Thalia skillfully guided the conversation toward Eurydice's cultural and scientific significance, extracting insights into the

UIA's motives and expectations for their journey into the cosmic unknown.

Unbeknownst to Zara, Thalia's inquiries subtly probed the vulnerabilities of their mission. The subtle interplay between the two friends, one driven by genuine curiosity and the other cloaked in the shadows of manipulation, added a layer of complexity to the preparations for the impending journey. The UIA's unwitting generosity in sharing the details of their cosmic ambitions unknowingly fueled the strategic advantage of the looming Terran Empire.

As the UIA prepared for the journey to Eurydice, the renewed connection between Zara and Thalia masked the shadows of manipulation. The race to Eurydice, now marked by intricacies of a past friendship and concealed motives, unfolded beneath the veneer of renewed camaraderie.

Shadowed Prelude: Cosmic Machinations

In the clandestine depths of the Terran Empire's secure communication hub, Thalia, operating under the guise of Agent Xerion, skillfully transmitted the acquired information to the enigmatic leaders. The holographic interface flickered to life, revealing General Valeria Drakonov, Grand Vizier Synestra, Quintus Caelum, and Shadow Mistress Seraphina Nocturna.

"Agent Xerion," General Drakonov's voice resonated with authority, "report on the information gathered from the UIA's impending expedition to Eurydice."

Thalia, adopting the calculated demeanor of the shadowy operative, began to relay the details garnered from Zara's unwitting disclosures. She navigated through the intricacies of the UIA's fleet composition, the advanced technologies at their disposal, and the security measures protecting their mission. The holographic displays mirrored her words, visually representing the UIA's cosmic arsenal.

"As you can see," Thalia emphasized, "their fleet boasts highly advanced spacecraft equipped with cutting-edge propulsion and shielding technologies. Their AI-driven sentinel probes will serve as an early warning system, and their adaptive camouflage mechanisms pose a challenge for any potential threat."

Grand Vizier Synestra, her gaze sharp and calculating, interjected, "And the security protocols surrounding their communication channels?"

Thalia responded with precision, "Encrypted on multiple levels, with adaptive algorithms that change in real-time. The UIA has implemented stringent measures to safeguard their data transmissions."

Quintus Caelum, the head of the Imperial Science Directorate, leaned forward, his curiosity evident. "What of their approach to Eurydice? How do they plan to navigate the unique challenges of the planet's topography?"

Thalia elaborated on Zara's descriptions, detailing the UIA's strategy for surveying the surface, pinpointing sites of interest, and addressing the challenges posed by the alien planet. The holographic representation of Eurydice became a strategic map, offering the Terran Empire a glimpse into the UIA's cosmic ambitions.

Shadow Mistress Seraphina Nocturna, the enigmatic head of the Imperial Intelligence Network, observed the holographic displays with a calculating gaze. "The UIA's motives and expectations for this mission, Agent Xerion, are they driven solely by scientific curiosity?"

Thalia, threading the narrative with subtle nuances, conveyed the UIA's pursuit of knowledge and cultural insights. "Their ambitions extend beyond scientific curiosity. There's a deeper resonance with Eurydice's cultural and historical significance, adding emotional weight to their cosmic endeavors."

General Drakonov, absorbing the information, leaned back in his chair. "Very well, Agent Xerion. Your insights are invaluable. Now, let us discuss our plan to eliminate the UIA once and for all."

The holographic displays shifted, revealing a strategic overview of Eurydice and the UIA's impending expedition. The Terran Empire leaders, emboldened by the intelligence gleaned from Thalia's clandestine efforts, gathered around the holographic table, their faces shrouded in a shadowy determination.

General Valeria Drakonov, Supreme Commander of the Terran Empire, studied the holographic projections with a calculating gaze. "We have a unique opportunity to cripple the UIA once and for all," she declared, her voice resonating with the authority that came with military prowess. "The UIA is marching toward Eurydice, oblivious to the storm we're about to unleash."

Grand Vizier Synestra, the chief political advisor, leaned forward, her eyes narrowing with strategic insight. "We must strike swiftly and decisively. The element of surprise is our greatest weapon. We can systematically dismantle their defenses once their fleet is scattered and in disarray."

Quintus Caelum, head of the Imperial Science Directorate, interjected with a sinister gleam in his eyes. "Let's not forget the technological advantage we've gained. We know their strengths and weaknesses. Our weaponry can be calibrated to exploit every vulnerability."

Shadow Mistress Seraphina Nocturna, the enigmatic head of the Imperial Intelligence Network, observed the holographic map with a predatory aura. "Agent Xerion has proven invaluable. With her guidance, we can predict their movements and be one step ahead. Victory is within our grasp."

As the discussion unfolded, battle plans were meticulously devised. The Terran Empire leaders strategized to intercept the UIA fleet on the outskirts of Eurydice, catching them in a cosmic pincer. The element of surprise, coupled with superior firepower, would be their trump card.

Yet, as the plans took shape, a subtle shift occurred among the leaders. General Drakonov, her gaze cold and calculating, proposed an unexpected twist. "Let them think they've won," she suggested. "Allow the UIA to establish their infrastructure on Eurydice. Once they're complacent, we strike. Their illusion of victory will crumble, replaced by the crushing defeat that awaits them."

The idea rippled through the room, the leaders exchanging knowing glances. The decision was made. The Terran Empire would let the UIA win the initial race and build their colonies. Then, when the time was ripe, they would unleash a devastating assault, ensuring the annihilation of the UIA's cosmic ambitions. The cosmic chessboard had been set, and the pieces were moving with calculated precision toward an inevitable confrontation.

General Valeria Drakonov's voice resonating with the gravity of impending conflict declared, "This, my esteemed comrades, shall be known as The Great War. A war that transcends the boundaries of the cosmos, where the Terran Empire asserts its dominance over the feeble UIA. Victory in this celestial battleground will be our legacy, etching our dominion across the stars for eternity. Let the UIA revel in their illusory triumph, for it shall be short-lived. The Great War will be our crucible, forging our destiny as the unquestioned masters of the universe." Her proclamation echoed through the dimly lit chambers, sealing the fate of the impending cosmic clash.

As General Valeria Drakonov's ominous declaration echoed through the clandestine chambers, Thalia, shrouded in the guise of Agent Xerion, felt a chilling resonance within. The weight of her actions, masked by her role, bore a heavy burden on her conscience. The proclamation of The Great War painted the impending conflict in hues of darkness. Thalia couldn't escape the realization that she had become an unwitting architect of the cosmic upheaval about to unfold. Her connection to Zara, entwined with shadows of a shared past, made the impending conflict a personal struggle. Hidden behind the mask, Thalia grappled with conflicting emotions, torn between the loyalty to the Terran Empire and the lingering echoes of a friendship that had now morphed into a cosmic confrontation.

As the weight of the impending conflict pressed upon her, Thalia's visage betrayed a subtle, devious smile, a glimpse of the darkness within asserting its control over her intricate dance of loyalty and manipulation.

A Colony Unveiled

The UIA headquarters on Aurora Beta hummed with the intensity of purpose as Zara took the reins of a grand endeavor—the establishment of a new colony on Eurydice. An orchestrated symphony of activities unfolded around her, with engineers fine-tuning blueprints and logistical coordinators ensuring the seamless execution of the ambitious plan. Holographic displays illuminated the vast potential of the alien planet, projecting visions of modular habitats and orbital platforms that would soon dot its surface.

Zara stood at the forefront of the bustling headquarters, her new crew assembled for an initial meeting in the briefing room. Dr. Alyssa Vega, a luminary in xenobiology, Commander Ethan Hale, a seasoned military strategist, and Chief Engineer Ravi Singh, a technological virtuoso, were among the diverse array of experts gathered. Each member brought a wealth of knowledge, and as Zara addressed the team, a sense of purpose permeated the room.

"Welcome, everyone. Our mission is twofold: to explore Eurydice's mysteries and establish a sustainable colony. We have a challenging road ahead, but with your expertise, I'm confident we can turn this alien world into a new home for humanity."

The team, a tapestry of scientific minds and strategic brilliance, engaged in discussions that shaped the trajectory of their mission. Plans for resource allocation, habitat construction, and cutting-edge scientific research unfolded. Zara's optimism echoed in the room, fueled by the collective spirit of the team and their shared vision to transform Eurydice into a beacon of hope for the future of humanity.

As the diverse team immersed themselves in the discussions, a meticulous tapestry of plans began to unfold, weaving together the collective expertise of scientific minds and strategic brilliance. The first thread of this intricate design was resource allocation, a strategic endeavor to harness the abundant resources of Eurydice for the benefit of the burgeoning colony. Geologists and surveyors collaborated to identify prime locations for resource extraction, ensuring a sustainable supply chain that would fuel the colony's growth.

Simultaneously, plans for habitat construction took shape, with architects, engineers, and environmental specialists collaborating to design modular habitats that could withstand the unique challenges of Eurydice. These habitats, equipped with cutting-edge technology, aimed not only to provide shelter but also to create a harmonious coexistence with the alien environment. Sustainable energy sources, advanced life support systems, and adaptable architecture became keystones in the endeavor to forge a human presence on the mysterious planet.

The most captivating aspect of the discussions centered around cutting-edge scientific research. Zara's vision for Eurydice went beyond survival; it aspired to unravel the profound mysteries concealed within the planet's depths. Scientists proposed innovative experiments to study the native flora and fauna, deciphering their biology and potential applications for the colony's benefit. Xenobiologists and ecologists sought to understand the intricate ecosystems, pushing the boundaries of human knowledge.

Moreover, the team envisioned deploying robotic probes equipped with state-of-the-art instruments to delve into the secrets of Eurydice's subterranean layers. Uncharted territories awaited exploration, and the scientific community eagerly anticipated the unprecedented discoveries that lay beneath the surface. The pursuit of knowledge became a driving force, propelling the team toward the frontiers of discovery and setting the stage for a new chapter in human exploration.

As the discussions unfolded, the plans for resource allocation, habitat construction, and cutting-edge scientific research crystallized into a comprehensive strategy. The team, fueled by a shared passion for exploration and discovery, stood ready to embark on a journey that would shape the future of humanity on Eurydice and illuminate the vast unknowns of the cosmos.

In the midst of the bustling preparations for the new colony on Eurydice, Zara dedicated herself to a multifaceted approach, ensuring the security and success of the mission while preserving the invaluable knowledge housed within the mysterious bunker. Her experiences on Eurydice had forged a strategic mindset, and she approached each aspect with meticulous planning.

First and foremost was the paramount concern of security. The haunting echoes of the past battle lingered in Zara's consciousness, a stark reminder of the vulnerability they faced in the cosmic unknown. She liaised closely with Commander Ethan Hale, the seasoned military strategist in her new crew, to fortify the defense protocols. Advanced surveillance systems, strategic placement of security outposts, and rigorous training exercises became integral components of their security strategy. Zara was resolute in her commitment to ensuring the colony's and its inhabitants' safety. She could never let the Terran Empire have victory again.

Simultaneously, Zara devised plans for exploring and documenting the enigmatic depths of Eurydice. Drawing from her previous encounters, she recognized the need for a balanced approach combining scientific curiosity and strategic caution.

Geologists and archaeologists collaborated to chart the planet's terrain, identifying prime locations for exploration and excavation. Zara, equipped with cutting-edge scanning devices, led scouting missions to analyze the surface composition and map potential points of interest.

The bunker, containing the cosmic revelations she had previously unearthed, held a place of paramount importance in Zara's preparations. She assembled a specialized team of engineers and scientists to develop protective measures for the bunker, shielding it from external threats and environmental hazards. Security protocols were established to regulate access, ensuring the knowledge within remained safeguarded.

Moreover, Zara sought collaboration with the Imperial Science Directorate, fostering an alliance to share information and insights. While her intentions were rooted in the spirit of cooperation, Zara remained vigilant, recognizing the delicate balance between collaboration and the potential for betrayal. The shadows of Thalia's past involvement compelled Zara to approach interstellar alliances with cautious optimism.

As the preparations intensified, Zara found herself at the intersection of responsibility and opportunity. The cosmic odyssey that awaited her and her team held the promise of profound discoveries and challenges. The culmination of strategic security measures, exploration plans, and protective protocols encapsulated Zara's dedication to charting a course that not only unveiled the mysteries of Eurydice but also ensured a resilient future for humanity on this alien world.

Finally, the day arrived; it was the dawning of a new era for Eurydice.

Eurydice Begins Anew

The dawn of a new era illuminated the surface of Eurydice as the seeds of humanity's presence took root. The preparations meticulously laid out by Zara and her team materialized into the establishment of the colony, with modular habitats rising against the alien landscape like beacons of human resilience. The hum of activity echoed across the planetary expanse as engineers fine-tuned the infrastructure, scientists calibrated their instruments, and the first settlers marveled at the cosmic horizon that stretched before them.

As the colony on Eurydice flourished, Zara couldn't help but feel a sense of relief mingled with satisfaction. The security measures put in place, the collaboration with the Imperial Science Directorate, and the strategic planning had seemingly borne fruit. The absence of any sign of the Terran Empire provided a momentary respite, a semblance of tranquility in the cosmic chaos that often enveloped their endeavors.

Yet, beneath the veneer of relief, an uneasy undercurrent tugged at Zara's consciousness. While comforting on the surface, the absence of the Terran Empire raised questions that echoed in the corridors of her mind. Had the Empire chosen to bide their time, observing from the shadows before making their move? Or, in an unexpected twist of fate, had they abandoned their pursuit of Eurydice altogether?

Zara, ever the vigilant explorer, couldn't shake the feeling that the calm preceding the storm could be more ominous than it seemed. The cosmic dance between the UIA and the Terran Empire had taken unexpected turns in the past, and the absence of conflict only fueled the apprehension that it might be the precursor to a more intricate stratagem.

She convened meetings with her security team, reviewing surveillance data and fortification protocols. Despite the lack of immediate threat, Zara maintained a stance of unwavering vigilance, recognizing that the cosmic tapestry often unfolded in unpredictable patterns. Her uneasy feeling, born from the lessons of the past, served as a constant reminder that the vast unknown held secrets that transcended even the most meticulous preparations.

Zara, recognizing the delicate balance between exploration and security, convened comprehensive meetings that brought together her security team and key members of the Imperial Science Directorate (ISD). The ISD, a crucial arm of the United Interstellar Alliance (UIA), was entrusted with the responsibility of advancing scientific knowledge, safeguarding cosmic discoveries, and fortifying humanity against external threats.

The ISD, under the leadership of Quintus Caelum, the head of the Imperial Science Directorate, played a multifaceted role in securing the universe. Its scientists were pioneers in groundbreaking research and strategists in deciphering potential threats. The collaboration between the ISD and the UIA's security forces was vital in navigating the complexities of cosmic exploration, where the boundaries between scientific discovery and potential peril were often blurred.

In the wake of the UIA's establishment on Eurydice, the inexplicable absence of the Terran Empire became a focal point of concern. Reports from across the universe indicated a mysterious vanishing act by the Empire, leaving behind a cosmic void. The uncertainty surrounding their whereabouts and intentions cast an overarching shadow on the sense of relief that the UIA and its colonies initially felt.

The meetings convened by Zara delved into this cosmic mystery, with the ISD contributing insights from their vast network of scientific observation posts and deep-space probes. Dr. Caelum and his team shared data on the disappearance of Terran Empire outposts and the enigmatic traces they left behind. The absence of the Empire's presence everywhere in the universe, seemingly simultaneous and without a discernible pattern, puzzled even the most astute minds within the ISD.

As Zara's security team exchanged information with the ISD scientists, a growing concern emerged about a mysterious figure known as Agent Xerion. Whispers within the Directorate suggested that this individual, shrouded in secrecy and operating on the fringes of cosmic intelligence, could hold the key to understanding the enigma surrounding the Terran Empire. With its advanced technology and expertise, the ISD now faced the challenge of unraveling the mysteries of the vanished Empire and addressing the shadowy presence of Agent Xerion, all while fortifying humanity against potential cosmic adversities.

Zara listened intently to all the information as she stared at the activity outside the UIA headquarters. As the colony on Eurydice burgeoned with life and the promise of a cosmic frontier, the silence of the interstellar expanse above held the potential for both serenity and turmoil and in the delicate balance between the two, Zara remained poised, ready to navigate the cosmic currents that awaited them on this alien world.

Zara emerged from the high-security meeting room, the weight of strategic discussions lingering in the air like a cosmic resonance. The holographic projections of Eurydice and the UIA colony's vital installations gradually dissipated, leaving the room in a subdued glow. The tension of the discussions resonated in Zara's thoughts as she stepped into the bustling hub of the UIA headquarters on Eurydice.

The establishment of the colony had been a monumental achievement, a testament to the collective efforts of the UIA. Yet, amidst the success, an unexplored mystery beckoned beneath the surface—an ancient bunker concealing secrets that could potentially alter the course of humanity's cosmic journey.

Zara's gaze lingered on the sealed entrance to the bunker, a place she had deliberately cordoned off upon their initial landing. Security protocols had dictated caution, and the potential dangers within the enigmatic structure warranted prudence. With the colony thriving and the security apparatus in place, the time had come to unveil the mysteries hidden within the subterranean depths.

She assembled a team of experts, a combination of scientists, engineers, and security personnel, each selected for their specialized skills. The security measures were recalibrated, and the sealed entrance creaked open, revealing the threshold to the unknown.

The team descended into the bunker, their steps echoing in the silent corridors that had remained untouched for eons before Zara's previous discovery. The flickering glow of holographic displays illuminated the path ahead, casting shadows on the ancient walls adorned with alien symbols. Zara led with a sense of purpose, a cosmic explorer unraveling the enigma of a forgotten chapter in the universe's history.

The team navigated through the labyrinthine passages, uncovering hidden chambers and unlocking doors that had stood closed for countless centuries. The remnants of an advanced civilization unfolded before them—technology that surpassed their understanding, libraries of knowledge encoded in crystalline structures, and murals depicting cosmic events long lost to time.

As they delved deeper, the bunker revealed glimpses of its purpose: a repository of knowledge, a testament to an ancient civilization's pursuit of cosmic enlightenment. Awestruck by the revelations, Zara felt the weight of responsibility and the potential consequences of the discoveries awaiting them.

The expedition through the bunker became a journey through the annals of cosmic history. In this cosmic odyssey, the echoes of the past intertwined with the aspirations of the present. Zara, surrounded by a team of dedicated explorers, stood at the nexus of discovery, prepared to unravel the mysteries that lay hidden beneath the surface of Eurydice.

Zara, fueled by an insatiable curiosity and driven by her carefully assembled team's collective expertise, embarked on exploring the mysterious bunker beneath the surface of Eurydice. The chosen crew members represented the pinnacle of their respective fields, each bringing a unique set of skills that would prove invaluable in the intricate dance between exploration and revelation.

Commander Ethan Hale, an experienced military strategist, stood as the sentinel at the forefront, his keen tactical mind ready to navigate the labyrinthine depths of the bunker. Dr. Alyssa Vega, a renowned xenobiologist, added her insightful expertise, anticipating potential extraterrestrial surprises that might lurk within the confines of the ancient structure. Chief Engineer Ravi Singh, a visionary in spacecraft technology, would play a pivotal role in deciphering the intricate mechanisms that powered the hidden recesses of the bunker.

The exploration commenced with a meticulous approach, each step a deliberate progression into the unknown. The entrance, adorned with enigmatic symbols, unfolded into a network of interconnected corridors. Zara, her eyes scanning the surroundings, marveled at the alien architecture that seemed to defy the conventional laws of construction.

The team, armed with advanced scientific instruments and guided by the holographic displays provided by the Imperial Science Directorate, meticulously moved through the initial chambers. As they ventured deeper, unexpected discoveries awaited them. Hidden rooms, previously concealed by advanced cloaking technology, revealed themselves in response to Zara's presence as if the bunker itself recognized the curiosity of its explorers.

Her xenobiological instincts on high alert, Dr. Vega studied the unusual flora that adorned the walls of one chamber. These extraterrestrial plant formations, emitting a soft luminescence, hinted at the possibility of a symbiotic relationship with the ancient technology that surrounded them.

Commander Hale, ever vigilant, ensured the security protocols were in place as they moved further into the bunker's heart. The team's progress was methodical, guided by a balance between scientific inquiry and the readiness to face any unforeseen challenges that might arise.

Chief Engineer Singh, his technological acumen put to the test, interfaced with the bunker's control systems. As they navigated through hidden passages and decoded the ancient script that adorned the walls, the technology responded with a symphony of lights and holographic displays, providing glimpses into the forgotten history embedded within Eurydice.

The journey through the bunker became a testament to the interdisciplinary collaboration of the team. They uncovered rooms filled with archives of cosmic knowledge, libraries of information encoded in intricate patterns, and chambers that seemed to resonate with the very essence of the universe's creation.

As they advanced further, the bunker unfolded like a cosmic tapestry, each discovery more awe-inspiring than the last. The explorers, led by Zara's indomitable spirit and the collective brilliance of their diverse skills, stood on the precipice of revelations that could reshape the destiny of humanity in the cosmos.

A palpable sense of anticipation hung in the air as they approached the final chamber. The sealed door, adorned with enigmatic symbols, gave way to reveal a room bathed in an otherworldly glow.

A cluster of unknown war weapons awaited discovery in the heart of the chamber. Hovering above pedestals, they emanated a humming energy, casting an ethereal light that danced along the walls. Zara's eyes widened in awe and trepidation as she took in the sight. These weapons were unlike anything the universe had ever seen, a testament to the advanced technology of the ancient civilization.

The weapons were adorned with inscriptions in an unknown language and intricate patterns etched into the metallic surfaces. The team, a gathering of brilliant minds, exchanged puzzled glances. As they attempted to decipher the instructions embedded in the artifacts, the air buzzed with anticipation.

With a sense of foreboding, Zara stepped closer to one of the humming weapons, her fingers tracing the alien symbols. As she did, the room seemed to pulse with energy. Suddenly, a holographic projection materialized above the weapon, displaying a language of cosmic intricacy.

The symbols flickered, transforming into a face that sent shivers down Zara's spine. It was a fleeting image but undeniably familiar. Thalia's visage emerged within the holographic display, her eyes holding an enigmatic gaze that spoke of ancient secrets and cosmic mysteries.

Zara recoiled, her heart pounding with a mixture of fear and disbelief. The image vanished as quickly as it appeared, leaving the team in stunned silence. The weapons continued to hum, their energy resonating with an ominous aura that transcended the bounds of time.

The discovery was a double-edged sword—weapons of unimaginable power, coupled with the unsettling realization that the Terran Empire had sought these artifacts. Grappling with the implications, Zara knew that the ancient weapons were not just a cosmic marvel but a harbinger of undeniable danger. The room, once a beacon of discovery, now echoed with the whispers of an ancient civilization's secrets and the looming threat that the weapons held for the fate of the cosmos.

As the team continued their examination of the mysterious weapons, an eerie realization settled over them like a cosmic shroud. The unknown language etched into the metallic surfaces seemed to shift, almost imperceptibly, as if responding to the team's presence.

The team's collective gaze fixated on the newly formed inscriptions as the symbols rearranged into a coherent language. The metallic surfaces seemed to pulse with otherworldly energy as if the weapons themselves were awakening to the presence of those who dared to unveil their secrets. The air in the chamber grew heavy with a palpable sense of foreboding.

In the flickering light of the alien symbols, the team exchanged hesitant glances, realizing that they were on the precipice of a revelation that could alter the course of their mission and the fate of Eurydice. It was as if the very essence of the weapons sought to communicate, to reveal the dire purpose behind their creation.

In a moment of shared understanding, the team's experts in linguistics and ancient civilizations worked feverishly to decipher the inscriptions. The chilling truth gradually emerged—the weapons were not mere artifacts of advanced technology; they were, in fact, instruments of cataclysmic power. The inscriptions spoke of devastation on an unimaginable scale, a purpose so grave that it hinted at the desperation of a civilization facing cosmic extinction.

The apocalyptic nature of the weapons became hauntingly clear as the inscriptions detailed a last resort, a final gambit to rewrite the fabric of reality itself. Now united in a sobering realization, the team grappled with the weight of the ancient arsenal's intended purpose. The chamber echoed with the gravity of their discovery, and the alien inscriptions served as a chilling testament to the dire measures civilizations might take when confronted with the looming specter of cosmic annihilation.

Zara, her eyes narrowing with a mix of horror and understanding, felt the weight of the revelation settle upon her shoulders. The team exchanged uneasy glances, the gravity of their discovery sinking in. These were not merely advanced technologies but the harbingers of time's end.

Just as the implications of the weapons began to echo through the chamber, a flicker of light heralded the reappearance of the holographic projection. Thalia's enigmatic visage materialized again, her voice resonating through the room like a haunting melody.

"Zara," Thalia's voice echoed, dripping with mockery, "you've stumbled upon the instruments of cosmic annihilation. Clever, aren't they? Weapons forged at the precipice of oblivion, designed to rewrite the fabric of reality itself."

Both startled and angered by Thalia's sudden appearance, Zara demanded answers. "Thalia, what is the meaning of this? Why would an ancient civilization create weapons of such destruction?"

Thalia's form now materialized within the alien symbols, her features obscured by the ethereal glow. Her response carried a haunting calmness as if she had anticipated this moment. "Zara, the weapons were not meant for mere destruction. They are the keys to universal dominance, a power that transcends the limits of mere civilizations. In their wisdom, the Ancients sought to grasp the very fabric of existence, to bend reality to their will."

As Thalia spoke, a subtle note of bitterness crept into her words, born from a perception that had festered since their shared childhood. "You were always the favored one, Zara. The prodigy with dreams of exploration, the shining star in the eyes of our instructors. But what about me? The one who was unfairly relegated to the shadows? The darkness within me found solace in those shadows, and the Terran Empire offered the power I had long believed should rightfully be mine."

The revelation of Thalia's embittered past hung in the air like an ominous fog, casting a shadow over the unfolding cosmic drama. Zara's eyes narrowed, mixed emotions swirling within her—confusion, empathy, and a tinge of regret. "Thalia, we can find another way. We can stop the Empire together as friends."

Thalia's response carried a chilling certainty, her bitterness juxtaposed with an almost mournful tone. "It's too late for that, Zara. The choices were made long ago, and the shadows have grown too deep. The Empire's hunger for power is insatiable; now, it's a force that cannot be halted. The Great War has begun, and the echoes of our shared past will be drowned in the cosmic storm."

Thalia's presence dissipated with those cryptic words, leaving the team in the dimly lit chamber, surrounded by the humming artifacts of cosmic devastation. The seismic onslaught echoes continued reverberating through the bunker, a somber reminder of the cosmic struggle that had now unfolded in full force.

The revelation hung in the air like an ominous fog, shrouding the team in a mixture of dread and disbelief. Zara's eyes narrowed, a cocktail of frustration and anger simmering within her. "Universal dominance? Is that the Terran Empire's ultimate goal? To wield these weapons and subjugate entire galaxies?"

Thalia's response carried a chilling certainty. "The Terran Empire desires control, Zara. Control over the cosmic tapestry, control over the destinies of countless worlds. These weapons are but a tool, a means to an end in their pursuit of unbridled power. The Ancients understood the allure of such dominion, and now the Empire seeks to claim it for themselves."

Grappling with the weight of the revelation, Zara felt a surge of defiance. "We won't let that happen. The UIA will stand against the Terran Empire. We'll protect Eurydice and every civilization threatened by their ambitions."

Thalia's spectral form seemed to waver, a faint smile playing on her lips. "Your noble intentions, Zara, are but flickers in the encroaching darkness. The Great War has begun, and the Empire's reach is vast. You may resist, but the shadows will consume all in the end."

Thalia's presence dissipated with those cryptic words, leaving the team in the dimly lit chamber, surrounded by the humming artifacts of cosmic devastation.

Suddenly, as if the very foundation of Eurydice trembled beneath their feet, a seismic shockwave reverberated through the bunker. The ground quaked with an unsettling intensity, causing the team to stagger and clutch onto nearby surfaces for support. The distant echoes of the tremor hinted at an external force, something vast and powerful, beyond the confines of the subterranean chamber.

Zara, her eyes wide with realization, exchanged alarmed glances with her team. The revelation struck them like a bolt of cosmic lightning—the Empire had launched an assault on Eurydice. While confined within the depths of the bunker, the physical manifestation of the seismic assault left no room for doubt. The once serene and uncharted planet now bore witness to the destructive force of the Terran Empire's onslaught.

The eerie glow of the alien symbols in the chamber seemed to flicker in tandem with the chaotic vibrations from above, casting unsettling shadows on the faces of the team. Thalia's faceless voice, laced with a sinister triumph, echoed within the chamber. "It seems the Terran Empire has decided to make their presence known, Zara. The Great War has begun, and your feeble attempts to understand these weapons won't save you from the impending darkness."

Zara, grappling with the seismic aftershocks and the weight of the ancient weapons' revelation, felt an ominous chill crawl up her spine. The cataclysmic events unfolding on the surface were a testament to the Empire's ruthlessness, and the stark reality of the Great War now eclipsed the cosmic mysteries they had sought to unravel.

The Great War Begins

The air within the bunker grew tense as Zara, fueled by a mixture of urgency and dread, made the heart-wrenching decision to leave the safety of the underground sanctuary. The distant rumble of explosions reverberated through the metallic walls, signaling the onset of the Empire's ruthless assault. The once-secure haven now felt like a trap, and Zara knew that staying underground could mean missing the chance to influence the course of the battle. With a determined resolve, she gathered her team, each member aware of the peril that awaited them on the surface.

As they walked the corridors, a palpable tension gripped Zara's chest. The bunker door slid open, revealing a world that had once been a canvas of possibility, now marred by the horrors of war. The acrid smell of smoke and burning ozone invaded their senses, a stark reminder of the destruction that unfolded above ground. Zara's eyes widened as she beheld the sky, once serene, now ablaze with fiery trails from energy projectiles, each streak a testament to the overwhelming might of the Terran Empire's weaponry.

A moment of horror gripped Zara, the weight of the impending battle settling upon her shoulders. The once-pristine landscape now lay scarred, a stark contrast to the vibrant Eurydice she had known. But amidst the horror, a spark of determination flickered in Zara's eyes. She knew that she held the mantle of leadership in this chaotic symphony of destruction. As a seasoned explorer, she had faced the unknown. Still, this was a different kind of unknown—an enemy veiled in darkness and a war that threatened to extinguish the very essence of Eurydice.

The battlefield stretched before them, a theatre of cosmic tragedy. Zara steeled herself for the role she was destined to play. The metallic clang of armored boots against the scarred earth resonated with a symphony of conflict. With each step, Zara embraced the resolve to lead her crew in this desperate struggle for survival. The surface of Eurydice, now transformed into a battleground, awaited the clash of civilizations. Zara, burdened by the weight of her decisions, stepped forward to face the inevitable storm.

The once-pristine skies of Eurydice metamorphosed into a theatre of cosmic chaos, punctuated by the ominous glow of the Terran Empire's fleet. Towering Dreadnoughts, brimming with dark matter-infused weaponry and crowned with colossal energy projectors, dominated the celestial expanse. These massive flagships exuded an air of ominous authority, casting shadows upon the ravaged landscape below. Nimble and agile interceptors danced through the chaos with deadly grace, engaging UIA fighters in deadly aerial ballets. Meanwhile, the heavily armored

Destroyers, their hulls adorned with colossal cannons. These unleashed barrages painted the heavens with trails of devastation.

From the lofty vantage of orbit, the Empire's formidable ships discharged beams of energy infused with dark matter technology. Each strike was a precision assault, leaving trails of cosmic destruction in their wake. As these beams collided with the atmosphere, the very fabric of Eurydice seemed to warp and distort, structures disintegrating into particles of luminescent dust. The Empire's onslaught was as relentless as it was ruthless, an orchestrated symphony of devastation sparing no corner of the planet from its cataclysmic reach.

The hum of Empire spacecraft, a haunting melody of impending doom, reverberated alongside the thunderous roars of destructive weaponry. Shockwaves from orbital bombardments shook the ground, creating seismic tremors that resonated through the battered landscape. Evading retaliation with uncanny precision, the Empire's fleet utilized advanced cloaking technology and intricate maneuvering patterns. UIA fighters struggled to lock onto their elusive adversaries; their attempts at a counteroffensive met with swift and calculated resistance.

The once-vibrant sky now pulsed with ominous hues, casting an eerie glow across the battlefield.

The cosmic tableau unfolded with surreal detail—
a ballet of destruction set against the backdrop of
the universe. As Eurydice's defenders fought
valiantly against overwhelming odds, the Empire's
strategic mastery became evident in every
calculated move. The battle became a cosmic
symphony, each crescendo and diminuendo
echoing the fate of Eurydice, teetering on the
precipice of annihilation.

The relentless storm of the Empire forces
descended upon the surface of Eurydice with a
ferocity that shook the very foundations of the
planet. Colossal dropships adorned with the
emblem of the Terran Empire released waves of
troops whose armored boots struck the ground
with a symphony of destruction. The haunting
whirr of propulsion systems echoed through the
once-idyllic valleys, their descent a prelude to the
impending clash between the forces of oppression
and the defenders of freedom.

UIA ground forces, standing as the last bastion of
defense, faced the onslaught with determination
and dread. The rhythmic cadence of Empire boots
resonated through the valleys, creating a
dissonance that clashed with the natural harmony
of Eurydice. Once adorned with the ethereal
beauty of the planet's natural wonders, the
battlefield now bore witness to the brutal struggle
for survival. The desperate winds carried with them
the acrid scent of burning structures and

smoldering vegetation, mingling with the metallic tang of energy discharges that hung heavy in the air.

As the clash of civilizations unfolded on the once-pristine landscape, the very essence of Eurydice seemed to recoil against the intrusion. The cosmic symphony of chaos played out in vivid detail—the resounding booms of explosive impacts, the crackling of energy discharges, and the anguished cries of both defenders and invaders. The fate of Eurydice hung in the balance, its destiny tethered to the outcome of this brutal struggle that defied the inherent beauty of the universe.

Above the battlefield, the ominous glow of the Terran Empire's fleet continued to cast shadows upon the war-torn landscape. The celestial armada, a formidable force driven by the insatiable hunger for dominion, hovered with malevolent intent. From the heavens, the Empire orchestrated the ballet of destruction, each move calculated to bring Eurydice to its knees. The defenders, now locked in a desperate struggle, fought for their lives and the soul of the cosmic jewel they called home.

Caught off guard by the suddenness and ferocity of the Empire's assault, the Security Council convened in the heart of the UIA headquarters on Aurora Beta. The holographic displays flickered with real-time updates from Eurydice, revealing the chaotic dance of warfare that unfolded on the distant planet. Tension hung thick as council members, faces etched with concern, urgently debated the most effective strategies to counter the Empire's advance.

Admiral Janus, the head of the Security Council, barked orders and directives to the various divisions of the UIA's military. His grizzled visage displayed a blend of determination and urgency, understanding the gravity of the situation. The UIA's fleet, despite its skill and advanced technology, found itself dancing on the precipice of defeat against an adversary whose cunning exceeded expectations.

Real-time communications flooded the room as Zara, leading the charge on the surface of Eurydice, relayed updates to the council. Her voice, a steady beacon in the storm of chaos, coordinated with military commanders to implement rapid response measures. The Security Council, recognizing Zara's pivotal role in the unfolding battle, urgently tried to convey orders and strategic shifts to support her efforts.

Above Eurydice, the cosmic expanse became a tumultuous battleground, with UIA and Empire spacecraft engaged in intense dogfights. The sleek UIA fighters, agile and evasive, engaged their adversaries in aerial ballets, weaving through streaks of energy fire. The booms of exploding ships reverberated through the cosmic void, and shimmering trails of wreckage marked the ongoing struggle for supremacy.

On the planet's surface, UIA ground forces fought with unwavering resolve against the Empire's relentless advance. Automated turrets whirred as they targeted enemy units, artillery explosions resonated with thunderous concussions, and the rhythmic footsteps of armored soldiers echoed through Eurydice's varied terrain. Each hill, forest, and plateau became a contested battleground, the diverse landscapes turning into strategic assets or liabilities.

The Security Council, facing the grim reality of the Empire's ruthlessness and strategic prowess, sought to rally the UIA forces and form alliances amid the chaotic conflict. Sacrifices were made, and the destiny of Eurydice hung precariously in the balance. The council urgently tried to establish a cohesive defense strategy, exploring every avenue to turn the tide against an adversary whose motives remained enigmatic, hidden in the dark recesses of the cosmic unknown.

Amidst the chaos of the ongoing battle, Zara's urgent pleas echoed through the chambers of the Security Council on Aurora Beta. The holographic displays, still flickering with the tumultuous scenes from Eurydice, became the backdrop to her impassioned appeal.

"Admiral Janus, Council members, we're facing an enemy with firepower we can't match. But there's something in the bunker, something the Ancients left behind. It's a gamble, I admit, but it might be our only chance. We can't afford to lose Eurydice," Zara implored, her eyes reflecting determination and desperation.

Though aware of the potential risks, Admiral Janus understood the gravity of the situation. "Zara, we need more than a gamble. We need a game-changer. What's in that bunker, and can it turn the tide?"

Zara hesitated for a moment, uncertainty crossing her features. "I found powerful weapons, but I don't know the extent of their destructive capability. The Ancients labeled them as instruments of cataclysmic power, designed for a last resort. If we use them, we're venturing into the unknown."

Council members exchanged wary glances, the weight of the decision palpable. After a tense silence, Admiral Janus spoke, "Zara, you have the council's authorization to return to the bunker and use those weapons. We're putting the fate of Eurydice in your hands."

As Zara received the green light, relief and apprehension washed over her. The battle raged on outside, and the uncertainty of what awaited her in the bunker hung like a specter. "I won't let you down," she vowed, determination in her voice.

As the holographic displays flickered, the scenes from Eurydice's surface painted a grim tableau of chaos and devastation. The once-pristine landscapes were marred by the relentless clash between the UIA and the Terran Empire. Streaks of energy projectiles lit up the skies, and the distant echoes of explosions reverberated through the holographic chamber.

Zara, standing amidst the luminous projections, absorbed the disheartening sights. The Security Council's authorization to return to the bunker had granted her a crucial opportunity. Still, the gravity of the situation weighed heavily on her shoulders. The holographic representations showcased the valiant efforts of UIA forces, their determination evident in the face of overwhelming odds.

As Zara prepared to embark on the perilous journey back to the bunker, she couldn't shake the realization that each passing moment intensified the struggle on Eurydice's surface. The holographic displays offered glimpses of the uneven battle—UIA fighters engaged in desperate dogfights, ground forces entrenched in fierce combat, and the ominous presence of the Terran Empire's fleet casting shadows over the beleaguered planet.

The urgency of the situation fueled Zara's determination. She knew that every second counted, and the fate of Eurydice hung in the balance. The journey ahead would be fraught with challenges, from navigating through the chaos on the surface to the unknown dangers lurking within the bunker itself.

With a resolute nod, Zara turned away from the holographic displays, leaving behind the dynamic scenes of war. The hum of activity within the UIA headquarters starkly contrasted with the grim realities unfolding on Eurydice. As she made her way to the embarkation point, a mix of emotions surged within her—hope, fear, and an unwavering resolve to confront the mysteries of the bunker and the ancient weapons it housed.

The holographic chamber, now silent, held the echoes of a decision that could shape the destiny of Eurydice and the UIA's struggle against the relentless onslaught of the Terran Empire. In the looming shadows of uncertainty, Zara stepped forward, ready to face the challenges that awaited her on the tumultuous journey back to the heart of the alien planet.

The fate of the UIA and Eurydice itself rested on her shoulders. The Security Council's decision was made amidst the chaos of war, and Zara now faced the daunting task of reaching the bunker before the relentless onslaught of the Terran Empire could thwart her mission.

Labyrinth of Deception

Amid the chaotic battleground on Eurydice's surface, Zara's desperate search for a weapon that could turn the tide revealed a grim reality. The arsenal at her disposal offered little in the face of the Empire's overwhelming force. She scoured the remnants of a fallen outpost, hoping to find a technological marvel that could match the prowess of the Empire's destructive weaponry. Alas, the debris yielded no such discoveries.

As despair threatened to consume her, Zara's gaze fell upon a forgotten relic—a cloaking cape tucked away in a dusty corner. The fabric whispered promises of stealth and evasion, yet Zara hesitated. The Empire was notorious for countering such devices. Though an intriguing find, the cloak seemed like a frail defense against the relentless might of the Empire.

In a moment of introspection, Zara leaned back against a decaying wall, her mind drifting to the lessons instilled by her parents. Memories of ancient battles and tales of cunning commanders who had navigated treacherous landscapes surged to the forefront of her thoughts. Then, a solution emerged, inspired by the wisdom of ages past. The tunnels and rugged terrain of Eurydice's landscape, a silent witness to a distant conflict etched in the planet's history, beckoned to her.

Zara's mind delved into the annals of history, retracing the footsteps of a legendary conflict that had unfolded centuries before on a distant world. The war, known as the Battle of Celestria Prime, held a storied place in the collective memory of strategic warfare. Celestria Prime, a planet of rich resources and strategic importance, had become the stage for a struggle that shaped the very essence of interstellar conflicts.

At the heart of the conflict was a brilliant commander, General Seraphina Voss, whose ingenuity and tactical acumen were etched into the annals of military history. The opposing force, a formidable coalition of rival factions known as the Galactic Hegemony, sought to assert dominance over Celestria Prime. Outnumbered and outgunned, General Voss faced an existential threat to her people.

In the face of overwhelming odds, General Voss turned to the natural formations of Celestria Prime—a planet adorned with towering mountain ranges, vast deserts, and intricate cave systems. Recognizing the value of exploiting the terrain to her advantage, she orchestrated a series of ambushes and hit-and-run tactics that left the Hegemony bewildered and disoriented. The conflict soon earned its name as the "Stratagem Wars," a testament to the clever strategies employed by General Voss.

The Stratagem Wars became a symbol of resilience and resourcefulness, showcasing how a clever commander could use the environment to offset numerical and technological disadvantages. The conflict ultimately ended with the Hegemony's withdrawal, defeated by a commander whose mastery of terrain had become legendary.

As Zara embraced the echoes of the Stratagem Wars, she drew inspiration from the indomitable spirit of General Seraphina Voss. The lessons of exploiting natural formations to outmaneuver a superior force resonated deeply, offering a glimmer of hope in the dire circumstances of Eurydice's current battle—The Great War.

With newfound determination, Zara embraced the ancient tactics that had once shaped the course of history. Now donned with purpose, the cloak became a tool in her arsenal. The battle-weary commander ventured into the subterranean labyrinth of tunnels and caverns, relying on the age-old art of surprise and guile. As the symphony of warfare raged above, Zara's steps resonated with the echoes of a bygone era, intertwining the past with the present in a desperate bid for survival.

The ancient tactics that had turned the tide in the Battle of Celestria Prime now beckoned to her as a glimmer of hope in the darkness of the Terran Empire's onslaught. Determined to employ these strategies, she knew she needed a team capable of executing these maneuvers with precision.

Navigating the war-torn landscape, Zara sought out individuals who shared her vision and understood the significance of the ancient stratagems. Her first recruit was Captain Alexei Valenkov, a seasoned military strategist known for his adaptability in unconventional warfare. Together, they ventured into the midst of the conflict, dodging energy beams and evading Empire patrols to assemble a team.

Next in line was Dr. Elara Lin, a brilliant geologist and expert in terrain analysis. Elara's knowledge of Eurydice's natural formations would be invaluable in identifying locations suitable for ambushes and strategic retreats. Despite the dangers, she joined Zara's cause, fueled by a shared commitment to employing every advantage the planet offered.

The team expanded to include Lieutenant Raj Singh, an expert in covert operations and infiltration. His skills in navigating through hostile territories made him a crucial asset in executing hit-and-run tactics. As they moved through the battlefield, Zara's team became a beacon of hope amidst the chaos, rallying like-minded individuals who saw the potential in ancient strategies to turn the tide against the Empire.

Their journey to reach the bunker was fraught with peril. Skirting enemy patrols and utilizing the landscape as cover, they ventured deeper into the heart of the conflict. Along the way, they encountered survivors of the UIA ground forces, individuals desperate for a glimmer of hope in the face of the Empire's overwhelming might. Zara's vision became a rallying point, a symbol of resistance against an adversary that seemed insurmountable.

Despite the risks and challenges, the team pressed on; each member was driven by the belief that the ancient stratagems could be the key to not only survival but a decisive counterstrike against the Empire. The echoes of General Seraphina Voss's legacy spurred them forward, a beacon of inspiration in a galaxy gripped by the turmoil of war.

As Zara navigated the treacherous terrain, she drew inspiration from historical battles and guerrilla warfare. Utilizing the natural features of Eurydice's diverse landscapes, she led her team through winding canyons, dense forests, and rocky plateaus. The UIA forces, under Zara's guidance, employed hit-and-run tactics, exploiting the uneven topography to their advantage.

The ancient art of camouflage became a valuable ally. Zara and her team blended into the shadows of the alien vegetation, using adaptive cloaking devices to evade the keen sensors of Empire reconnaissance. Like shadows in the night, they moved silently, avoiding direct confrontation whenever possible and striking with precision when the opportunity arose.

Zara's knowledge of ancient communication methods also played a crucial role. Employing coded signals reminiscent of past civilizations, she orchestrated coordinated movements, allowing UIA squads to communicate discreetly and coordinate ambushes. The echoes of ancient strategies reverberated through the chaos of the modern battlefield.

Zara employed diversionary tactics as they encountered Empire patrols, drawing attention away from her main route to the bunker. Decoys and holographic illusions confounded the Empire forces, creating illusions of multiple UIA movements and confusing their tracking systems. The once-clear distinctions between reality and illusion blurred in the heat of battle.

The vast underground networks of caves and tunnels provided Zara with an ancient advantage. Exploiting her knowledge of these subterranean pathways, she led her team through hidden passages, avoiding direct confrontations with the overwhelming Empire forces on the surface. These ancient tunnels became a labyrinthine refuge, shielding the UIA forces from the prying eyes of the Empire.

The battle on Eurydice became a dance between the past and the present, where ancient tactics met cutting-edge technology. Zara's resourcefulness and historical insights became a beacon of hope in the face of overwhelming odds. Each step brought her closer to the heart of the planet and the mysterious bunker that held the potential to alter the course of the Great War.

As the remnants of the UIA forces and Zara's team converged on the vicinity of the bunker, the distant silhouette of the Terran Empire's advanced troops came into view. The strategic advantage of the natural formations and tunnels provided a fleeting moment of hope. Still, the proximity of the enemy demanded an in-close engagement. A hushed determination settled among Zara's team as they prepared for the inevitable clash, their resolve tested in the crucible of war.

The battle unfolded in the shadow of the ancient stratagems. Captain Alexei Valenkov, leading the charge with tactical brilliance, orchestrated ambushes and hit-and-run maneuvers, momentarily gaining the upper hand. Dr. Elara Lin, utilizing her geological expertise, identified strategic chokepoints, enabling the team to control the flow of the battle.

Lieutenant Raj Singh, a master of covert operations, engaged in fierce close-quarter combat, dispatching Empire soldiers with lethal precision. Despite the odds, the Empire's relentless advance took its toll. The air crackled with energy discharges, and the echoing sounds of gunfire and explosions resonated through the labyrinthine terrain.

As the battle raged, the team faced the harsh reality of war. Some fell, sacrificing themselves to buy precious moments for their comrades. The once-unyielding resolve of Lieutenant Raj Singh wavered as he fought valiantly, succumbing to the overwhelming force of the Empire. Dr. Elara Lin, too, faced the brutality of close combat, her scientific mind adapting to the chaos of war.

Amidst the carnage, Captain Alexei Valenkov, battered but resolute, continued to lead the charge. Fighting alongside her remaining team members, Zara carried the weight of loss on her shoulders. The air thickened with grief and determination as the team pressed forward, inching closer to the bunker that held the potential to change the course of the Great War. The sacrifice of those who had fallen became the rallying cry for those who remained, a testament to the indomitable spirit of humanity in the face of cosmic adversity.

The battle's crescendo echoed through the ravaged landscape as Zara and the remnants of her team fought their way toward the bunker. The once-hidden entrance came into view, but the door damaged and partially blocked by debris from the intense firefight, posed a formidable obstacle. Time was a luxury they couldn't afford, and desperation fueled Zara's determination to breach the bunker's protective threshold.

With a grim glance at her surroundings, Zara noticed an ancient relic—a colossal tree trunk toppled during the chaos of battle. The massive roots, now exposed, crisscrossed the entrance, creating a natural barricade. The tactical genius of centuries past sparked an idea in Zara's mind. She directed her remaining team to clear the debris, revealing the intricacies of the tree's roots.

Using their combined strength, they manipulated the roots, weaving them into a makeshift battering ram. Fueled by a sense of urgency, the team thrust the improvised ram against the damaged door. Resilient and unyielding ancient roots exerted tremendous force, gradually splintering the barrier that denied them entry.

As they reached the entrance and Zara rushed in, a sudden force slammed the bunker door shut, separating Zara from her team. Darkness enveloped her, but the urgency of the situation fueled Zara's resolve. Despite the unknown force that had sealed the entrance, she knew she had to navigate the dimly lit corridors alone and reach the weapons of destruction she had uncovered—an ancient arsenal that held the potential to alter the course of the Great War. The echoes of her footsteps reverberated through the bunker as Zara pressed forward into the unknown, driven by a determination that transcended the confines of the subterranean sanctuary.

In the oppressive darkness of the bunker's corridors, Zara pressed forward, her senses heightened by the absence of light. Each step was calculated, a blend of muscle memory and the resolute determination that had guided her through countless challenges. The labyrinthine passages seemed to stretch endlessly, but Zara drew upon her training, navigating the unseen obstacles with a grace borne of necessity.

The echoes of distant battle reverberated through the bunker, a constant reminder of the perilous world beyond its sealed confines. Zara's fingers brushed against cold metal walls as she moved forward, her every sense attuned to the task at hand. Her training echoed in the quiet recesses of her mind, guiding her through the unseen twists and turns.

As Zara continued her solitary journey, a distant glimmer of light emerged. The doorway to the room containing the ancient weapons was finally in sight. Relief, albeit momentary, washed over her. The anticipation of reaching the arsenal that held the power to tip the scales in the Great War fueled Zara's resolve.

With cautious steps, she entered the room, the darkness yielding to a dim glow that emanated from the ancient artifacts within. The weapons, enigmatic and powerful, rested in their dormant state. Zara's gaze swept across the room, assessing the instruments that could reshape Eurydice's destiny. It was a momentary respite, a breath caught between the relentless beats of war. At that moment, Zara gathered herself for the challenges that awaited. Little did she know that the shadows within the room held a more profound threat, one that would test her determination and the very fabric of her existence.

Dual of Destiny

In the dimly lit chamber, Zara's hand reached towards the gleaming console housing the weapons of destruction, anticipation, and hope coursing through her veins. The air hung heavy with the weight of destiny when the echo of Thalia's voice interrupted the silence.

"You think you can unlock the power within these relics, Zara?" Thalia's disembodied voice reverberated through the room, a taunting melody that seemed to dance between the shadows. Zara's eyes darted around, scanning the darkness for any sign of her elusive adversary.

"Thalia, show yourself! If you have something to say, say it to my face," Zara demanded, her tone a blend of determination and frustration. The metallic walls seemed to absorb her words, leaving an eerie silence in their wake.

As Zara continued to scrutinize the room, the air crackled with an unsettling energy, and the tension escalated with each passing second. The weapons, tantalizingly close, stood as silent witnesses to the impending confrontation. The stage was set for a duel that would determine the fate of galaxies, a clash between former friends turned bitter adversaries.

Thalia's ghostly voice continued its haunting melody in the suffocating darkness, mocking Zara's essence. "Oh, Zara, the great leader. Your leadership led your entire crew to their demise once, and now, here you are again—alone, abandoned, and clinging to false hope." Thalia's words echoed with a venomous resonance, each syllable a cruel reminder of past failures.

Zara gritted her teeth, her fists clenching in frustration as she demanded, "Enough of these games, Thalia! Show yourself!"

Thalia's voice chuckled malevolently. "You always were blind to the truth, weren't you? Blind to your own weaknesses and blind to the weaknesses of those who followed you. A leader destined for failure."

Zara's jaw tightened, her patience wearing thin, but she held onto her composure. "Enough hiding. Face me!" she demanded once more.

In a sudden surge of anger, Zara turned the tables. "I always knew you were weak, Thalia. Even back when we were kids. You were never strong enough to handle the challenges life threw at us. That's why you've resorted to shadows and deceit." Zara's words cut through the darkness, a calculated strike at the heart of Thalia's insecurities.

In a furious explosion of energy, Thalia materialized, her form taking shape within the dimly lit chamber. A scream tore through the air as the once-disembodied voice manifested into a tangible, wrathful presence. The room crackled with tension as the two adversaries stood face to face, the ghosts of their shared past whispering of a destiny intertwined with betrayal and conflict.

As Zara reached for the weapon of destruction, Thalia's form rippled with a malevolent energy. With a vicious snarl, Thalia lunged, her movements a blur of predatory grace. The battle erupted in the dimly lit chamber, a clash of wills and desperation. Thalia's strikes were relentless, a storm of calculated ferocity aimed at breaking Zara's defense.

The room echoed with the harsh sound of blows, the clash of two once-friends now entangled in a bitter struggle. Fueled by determination, Zara countered each assault, her movements a dance of evasion and retaliation. The air crackled with energy as they circled each other, a cosmic tension building in the confined space.

As Thalia gained the upper hand, her blows landing with brutal precision, Zara felt the weight of impending defeat. With a surge of desperation, she activated the cloak, and in an instant, she disappeared from Thalia's grasp. The sudden disappearance left Thalia livid, her furious gaze scanning the empty air where Zara once stood.

The battle continued in the shadows, Zara utilizing the cloak's invisibility to strike from unexpected angles. The room became a battleground of uncertainty, Thalia raging against an adversary who could slip from her grasp. The brutality of the fight intensified a clash of light and darkness, echoing the cosmic struggle that unfolded beyond the confines of the bunker.

Amidst the pulsating hum of the ancient chamber, Zara's fingers brushed against the cool, metallic surface of the weapon of destruction. The room itself seemed to respond to her touch, the air charged with an otherworldly energy. Yet, victory was far from assured, for standing in her path was once again the disembodied form of Thalia, a bitter rival whose schemes spanned the cosmos.

"You think you can defy me, Zara?" Thalia's voice taunted, reverberating through the chamber. Zara, now cloaked in invisibility, scanned the room, trying to pinpoint Thalia's presence. The echoes of their childhood rivalry played out in the cosmic battleground, and Zara demanded, "Show yourself, Thalia! Face the consequences of your betrayal."

In response, Thalia's laughter echoed, mocking Zara's leadership and reminding her of her devastating loss on Eurydice. "You were always destined to fail, Zara. Alone, just like you were back on that doomed mission." The taunts cut deep, reopening wounds of the past. Zara's determination, however, remained unshaken.

The cloak granted her a fleeting advantage, and Zara seized the moment to reach for the weapon. The chamber erupted in a burst of blinding light as the weapon responded to her touch. The battle took a turn, and Zara unleashed its power against Thalia. The room trembled with energy, and Thalia recoiled, her disembodied form flickering in the face of the weapon's might.

As the echoes of Thalia's laughter reverberated through the ancient chamber, the disembodied voice taunted Zara with menacing words that sent shivers down her spine. "You thought a mere cloak could protect you from the consequences of your choices, Zara? How naive! I've existed long before you, and I'll endure long after you're forgotten. This weapon, this feeble attempt at resistance, won't save you or your precious UIA."

Zara, invisible in her cloak, listened to Thalia's ominous words, feeling the weight of her adversary's disdain. Thalia's disembodied presence seemed to linger in the shadows, an ever-present threat that transcended the bounds of the physical realm. "You believe you can control the power within that weapon? How amusing. It will consume you, Zara, just as your own failures have. Eurydice will crumble, and your feeble attempts at defiance will be erased from the cosmic tapestry."

The hum of the weapon intensified as Zara's grip on it tightened. Thalia's voice took on a more sinister tone, whispering into the void of the chamber. "You're a pawn in a game you can't comprehend, Zara. The Terran Empire, the UIA, all mere puppets dancing to a cosmic symphony you can't even fathom. This futile struggle will be your undoing, and no cloak, no weapon, can shield you from the impending darkness."

As Zara grappled with the weight of Thalia's words, the disembodied voice grew more pronounced, an insidious presence that seemed to seep into the very fabric of her being. "Embrace your destiny, Zara, for you are nothing more than a fleeting spark in the grand inferno of the universe. The time for reckoning is upon you, and no amount of defiance can alter the cosmic design."

The weapon pulsed with energy, responding to the charged atmosphere within the chamber. Zara, still concealed by the cloak, stood resolute but haunted by the looming threat Thalia posed. The battle between former friends had escalated beyond the physical, delving into cosmic forces and ancient enmity. As the echoes of Thalia's words lingered, Zara braced herself for the challenges ahead, knowing that the true test of her mettle awaited on the war-torn surface of Eurydice.

The oppressive darkness seemed to coalesce in the pulsating silence that followed Thalia's foreboding words, giving birth to an eerie manifestation. Thalia's image materialized once more, bathed in an otherworldly glow, but this time, a malevolent aura surrounded her, an ominous darkness that transcended the familiar confines of the holographic projection.

Still concealed in her cloak, Zara felt a shiver run down her spine as the malevolence emanating from Thalia's image intensified. The once-familiar features of her childhood friend were now distorted by an inexplicable, chilling presence. Thalia's eyes once filled with curiosity and ambition, now glowed with an unholy fervor, a testament to the depths of her transformation.

As the darkness coiled around Thalia's form, a sensation of impending doom permeated the chamber. The air grew heavy, and Zara could almost taste the malevolence that radiated from the darkened silhouette before her. It was an evil, an ancient force that surpassed any semblance of Thalia she had known.

For a moment that felt like an eternity, the malevolent darkness enshrouded Thalia's image, creating an unsettling tableau. The ambient hum of the weapon seemed to synchronize with the ominous aura. This cosmic resonance echoed through the chamber.

Suddenly, as if whisked away by a shadowy tempest, Thalia's image vanished. The darkness receded, leaving Zara alone in the quiet chamber, her cloak still concealing her from the unseen forces at play. The lingering malevolence lingered in the air, an intangible reminder that Thalia's transformation had reached depths beyond comprehension.

As the echoes of Thalia's cryptic parting words resonated, Zara stood at the precipice of a cosmic struggle, the weight of her choices echoing through the ancient chamber. The weapon of destruction, pulsating with untold power, held the key to Eurydice's fate and the universe's destiny.

With Thalia temporarily defeated, Zara stood alone in the quiet aftermath. The weapon hummed with latent power, and the weight of its potential consequences bore heavily on Zara's shoulders. The battlefield outside awaited her return, and the fate of Eurydice hung in the balance. The decision to wield such destructive force against the Terran Empire rested squarely on Zara's shoulders. As she contemplated her next move, the echoes of Thalia's vow lingered, a stark reminder that the cosmic conflict was far from over.

The Weight of Destiny

The soft hum of the ancient weapon reverberated within the chamber, a symphony of cosmic resonance that transcended the boundaries of time and space. Zara, cloaked in the dim glow of the holographic displays, stood at the precipice of a monumental decision that would echo through the cosmos.

Surrounded by the pulsating energy of the ancient weapon, its ethereal light played upon Zara's features, casting an otherworldly sheen on her determined countenance. Once static and lifeless, the holographic displays now danced with celestial lights, projecting intricate patterns across the chamber. The very air seemed to vibrate with the power of the weapon she now possessed.

As Zara grappled with the weight of her decision, uncertainty hung in the air like a cosmic mist, swirling around her in undulating waves. The ancient weapon, a conduit to forces beyond comprehension, could shape Eurydice's destiny and the entire universe. The holographic displays flickered with glimpses of possible outcomes, each path branching into the vast expanse of the unknown.

The cosmic mist of uncertainty became a palpable presence, weaving through the chamber and whispering the echoes of countless futures. Zara's inner struggle was intricately entwined with understanding how the ancient weapon functioned. Its power lay in the delicate balance between creation and destruction, a dual essence that defied conventional understanding.

Zara's countenance bore the weight of responsibility and determination in the dim glow. Her eyes reflected the cosmic radiance of the ancient weapon, mirroring the choices that danced within the holographic projections. The symphony of cosmic resonance intensified, a melodic reminder of the profound impact a single decision could have on the tapestry of reality.

The struggle within Zara was not just against the uncertainty of the present but the daunting responsibility of comprehending the intricate mechanisms of the ancient weapon. It was a dance with the fundamental forces of the universe, a delicate choreography that required a profound understanding of the balance between creative genesis and devastating obliteration.

The ancient weapon, a double-edged sword of cosmic significance, awaited her command. In this celestial crucible, Zara's inner turmoil mirrored the cosmic forces at play. The chamber held its breath, suspended in anticipation of the momentous choice that would determine the fate of Eurydice and the vast expanse beyond.

As Zara grappled with the weight of her decision, uncertainty hung in the air like a cosmic mist. The holographic displays, once static, began to flicker with fragments of visions from the past as if the weapon itself sought to communicate its secrets. Amidst the spectral dance of lights, a familiar figure materialized—the ghostly form of General Seraphina Voss, a revered hero from the UIA's history.

Voss, a phantom from the Battle of Celestria Prime, conveyed enigmatic knowledge to Zara. The visions unfolded like fragments of a cosmic tapestry, revealing the intricate workings of the ancient weapon and the potential consequences of its activation. Zara's mind absorbed the cryptic insights, translating them into a newfound clarity that resonated with the cosmic hum in the chamber.

However, clarity brought with it the burden of responsibility. Zara found herself in possession of a weapon whose true power and capabilities remained shrouded in mystery. The holographic displays offered glimpses of celestial phenomena and arcane symbols, and Zara struggled to decipher their meaning. A wrong move could unleash catastrophic consequences on the Terran Empire and the UIA forces stationed on Eurydice.

Her mind became a battleground of doubt and determination, wrestling with the delicate balance between victory and destruction. The spectral figure of Voss lingered in the periphery, a silent guide urging caution and precision. The chamber, charged with cosmic energy, seemed to pulse in tandem with Zara's heartbeat as she deliberated the fate of Eurydice.

In this moment of uncertainty, Zara faced the daunting task of unlocking the true potential of the ancient weapon. Now a mosaic of celestial symbols, the holographic displays awaited her command. As the weight of responsibility settled on her shoulders, Zara steeled herself for the impending storm, ready to navigate the cosmic currents and forge a destiny that would resonate across the cosmos.

Armed with the spectral insights bestowed upon her by the vision from Voss, Zara emerged from the bunker, stepping into the maelstrom of chaos that unfolded above ground. The battleground stretched before her, a tumultuous tapestry of conflict painted in the fiery hues of energy discharges. The air crackled with the residue of cosmic warfare. Zara, a lone figure against the celestial backdrop, surveyed the scarred landscape. The fate of Eurydice beckoned, and with a resolute heart, Zara stepped into the crucible of destiny.

Stealth became Zara's ally in this cosmic ballet of destruction. The cloak, a shroud of invisibility gifted by ancient technology, enveloped her form, rendering her imperceptible to prying eyes. With each purposeful stride, she glided through the chaos of battle, a phantom navigating the contested terrain. Skirmishes erupted around her, the relentless advances of the Empire's forces deftly avoided as she moved with an almost ethereal grace.

Every silent step brought Zara closer to the looming silhouette of the Empire's control ship, the linchpin of their cosmic strategy. Amidst the chaos of battle, her mind raced through the corridors of memory, drawing upon the knowledge instilled in her during her rigorous training at the UIA program.

In the hallowed halls of the UIA, Zara had immersed herself in the intricacies of cosmic warfare, studying the distinctive profiles of various spacecraft and command ships. The program had equipped her with an unparalleled understanding of the diverse fleets that navigated the vast expanse of the universe. Each ship's class bore unique characteristics, from their hull design to the arrangement of their propulsion systems.

As she closed in on the Empire's armada, Zara's keen intellect sifted through the visual cacophony of battle. The command ship, a colossal presence amongst the swirling dance of vessels, bore the unmistakable hallmarks that her UIA training had etched into her memory. The arrangement of its towering structures and the resonance of its energy signatures coalesced into a distinct pattern that set it apart from the rest.

The cosmic tapestry unfolded before her, and in that moment, Zara's academic prowess metamorphosed into a practical skill that would decide the fate of Eurydice. She navigated the battlefield with a precision that transcended the chaos, her intuition guiding her unerring path toward the Empire's control ship.

The silent steps became purposeful strides, each bringing her closer to the linchpin of the Empire's strategy. Her gaze, honed by years of study and sharpened in the crucible of battle, locked onto the distinct contours of the control ship. There, amidst the cosmic tumult, Zara's past collided with the present as her UIA training seamlessly merged with the exigencies of war.

The looming silhouette, once an enigma in the vastness of space, now stood exposed to Zara's discerning eye. It was a testament to the symbiosis of her education and experience—an intersection of knowledge and intuition that positioned her as the vanguard against the encroaching tide of the Terran Empire.

The celestial tableau played out in a kaleidoscope of brilliance and devastation, a dance of lights and shadows. Zara's senses were heightened, attuned to the rhythmic ebb and flow of the cosmic energies that clashed around her. The control ship, a monolithic presence in the chaos, cast its ominous shadow over the battlefield. It was the nexus of the Empire's dominion, a strategic fulcrum upon which the fate of Eurydice pivoted.

As Zara approached the heart of the conflict, the cloak of invisibility began to weave its illusions with greater intensity. The very fabric of reality seemed to bend around her, concealing her presence from the watchful gaze of the Empire. The skirmishes intensified, a symphony of warfare echoing through the cosmos. Yet, Zara moved undetected, a silent force on a singular mission.

The fate of Eurydice hung in the balance, and Zara, armed with the spectral insights of General Seraphina Voss, embraced the weight of her cosmic destiny. The control ship loomed ever larger in her invisible journey, its dark silhouette a harbinger of the pivotal moment that would determine the course of the Great War. The crucible of destiny awaited, and Zara, a spectral presence in the cosmic theater, prepared to unveil the ancient weapon's power against the Empire's relentless onslaught.

The control ship, an imposing monolith adorned with ominous crimson lights, became the focal point of Zara's daring mission. Her strategic acumen led her through the maelstrom of battle, avoiding detection as she closed in on the heart of the Empire's command. The cosmic theater pulsed with tension, and Zara, driven by purpose, prepared to alter the course of the Great War with a weapon whose potential for devastation rested on her shoulders.

Evading detection, Zara made her way through the labyrinthine corridors of the control ship. The cloak of invisibility shielded her from the prying eyes of Empire forces as she delved into the heart of the cosmic behemoth. The silence of her infiltration was juxtaposed against the clamor of battle outside. The fate of Eurydice hung in the balance, and Zara pressed forward with determination and purpose.

The control ship's interior was a surreal blend of advanced technology and foreboding aesthetics. Zara navigated through sterile corridors and passed by rooms filled with uniformed Empire personnel, all oblivious to her presence. Her UIA training honed her strategic thinking and instilled in her an understanding of ship layouts and command structures.

As Zara approached the control room, the ancient weapon's hum resonated with her heartbeat's pulse. The anticipation of the impending encounter hung as she reached the entrance. The control room, a nexus of cosmic authority, awaited her presence. With a steady resolve, Zara stepped into the heart of the Empire's command, ready to unleash the weapon's power and reshape the destiny of Eurydice.

The control room was a sprawling chamber bathed in the eerie glow of holographic displays. Empire officers moved with purpose, their attention fixed on the ongoing battle, unaware that an intruder had breached their sanctum. Zara moved with the calculated grace of a ghost, weaving through the bustling personnel.

Her gloved hand hovered over the holographic interface as she reached the central console. The pulsating energy of the ancient weapon resonated with her every move. The UIA had equipped her with a profound understanding of the Empire's technological systems, allowing her to interface seamlessly with the control room.

As Zara's cloak of invisibility dissipated, revealing her presence to the unsuspecting Empire personnel, the control room plunged into a momentary hush. With her UIA-issued neural interface gloves, Zara swiftly activated a non-lethal neural disruptor function. The technology sent out focused electromagnetic pulses, temporarily incapacitating the Empire officers without causing any lasting harm.

In a blur of calculated movements, Zara disarmed and disabled the personnel in the control room.

Her training in close-quarters combat and the advanced technology at her disposal allowed her to neutralize potential threats swiftly and silently. The incapacitated Empire officers slumped to the ground, unconscious but alive.

With the immediate danger mitigated, Zara redirected her focus to the central console. The holographic displays flickered with vital information about the Empire's fleet and the ongoing battle. The hum of the ancient weapon intensified, reinforcing the gravity of the moment. Zara's fingers danced across the holographic controls, initiating the sequence to disable the ship's defenses.

As the cloak of invisibility served its purpose, allowing her to surprise and disarm the Empire personnel, Zara knew she needed to buy time to complete her mission. Drawing on her UIA training, she accessed the ship's security systems, initiating a holographic decoy program that projected false images of the control room to the security monitors. The ruse would provide a crucial window of confusion, diverting attention from her actual location for mere minutes.

Simultaneously, she activated an encrypted force field around the control console, creating a protective barrier against potential security breaches. The force field, a cutting-edge technology developed by the UIA, employed quantum encryption to resist even the most advanced Empire security protocols.

As alarms started blaring throughout the ship, signaling the breach in the control room, Zara maintained her focus on the task at hand. She manipulated the holographic controls with the neural disruptor engaged and the force field in place. The ancient weapon responded to her commands, and the Terran Empire's armada, unwittingly following her lead, veered away from Eurydice.

In the tense moments that followed, Zara's strategic prowess, enhanced by UIA technology, prevailed against the Empire's security measures. The control room, now a battleground of digital warfare, became the epicenter of a cosmic shift. The fate of Eurydice hung in the balance, and Zara, standing amidst incapacitated Empire personnel, pressed forward with determination and purpose.

With a final command, Zara redirected the ship's targeting systems. The once-formidable armada of the Terran Empire, now under her control, turned its destructive power away from Eurydice. The celestial battleground shifted as the Empire's forces, unwittingly following Zara's command, ceased their assault on the beleaguered planet.

As the dust settled on the cosmic canvas, Zara stood amidst the silent control room, a lone figure who had wrested command from the grasp of the Empire. The ancient weapon's hum echoed with a sense of triumph. Still, the test lay ahead—how to wield its power without succumbing to the same devastation it promised to unleash upon the Terran Empire.

Resonance of Destiny

The holographic displays in the control room flickered with the redirected trajectory of the Terran Empire's armada. The ancient weapon, now under Zara's command, resonated with cosmic energy as it altered the course of the looming threat away from Eurydice. The planet's fate hung in the balance. Encircled by the subdued Empire personnel, Zara knew her mission was far from over.

As the alarms continued to wail throughout the control ship, Zara made her way toward the exit, the pulsating energy of the weapon echoing her every step. The invisibility cloak enveloped her, providing a shield against potential security forces that might be rushing to reclaim the compromised control room. Yet, she knew the real battle awaited her on Eurydice's surface.

Exiting the control room, Zara navigated the labyrinthine corridors with the ancient weapon held securely at her side. The hum of the weapon seemed to harmonize with the moment's urgency. The real challenge lay ahead – redirecting the Empire forces engaged in battle on Eurydice.

Emerging from the control ship, Zara surveyed the ongoing battle below. The once-unrelenting advance of the Terran Empire's forces now faltered as confusion gripped their ranks. The redirected armada sailed away into the cosmic expanse, leaving Eurydice momentarily free from the imminent threat. However, the ground forces continued their ruthless assault, creating a stark contrast against the serene backdrop of Eurydice's natural beauty.

Zara descended to the surface, utilizing the cloak to infiltrate the contested zones unnoticed. The holographic displays embedded in the ancient weapon offered insights into the location of the Empire and UIA forces. Still, the lines between them blurred in the chaos of war.

A vision from General Seraphina Voss echoed in Zara's mind – the resonance of destiny. Voss had imparted the knowledge that the weapon could distinguish the intent of those it encountered. It resonated with the essence of those driven by aggression and conquest, identifying them as Empire forces.

However, the decision to wield the weapon was not without its weight. Zara hesitated, haunted by the memory of a previous battle where her decisions led to losing her entire crew. The ancient weapon promised a solution – an expansive surge of energy meant to incapacitate the Empire forces, sparing them from permanent harm. However, the dire circumstances left Zara with no choice but to grapple with the harsh reality that mercy had no place in the face of cosmic annihilation.

In a moment of contemplation before the dire decision to unleash lethal force, the ethereal figure of Commander Voss materialized in Zara's vision. The ghostly presence carried with it the weight of celestial wisdom, a testament to battles fought and destinies shaped. "Zara," Voss's voice echoed in the cosmic recesses of her mind, "the fate of Eurydice rests upon the precipice, and your choices will echo through the corridors of history. Remember that in the face of cosmic annihilation, a leader must navigate the shadows with a resolute heart. The cosmic tapestry awaits your stroke, and your legacy will be inscribed in the annals of time. Choose wisely, for the universe watches, and the threads of destiny hang in your delicate balance." With those words, the spectral vision dissipated, leaving Zara with newfound resolve as she confronted the harrowing decision that would determine the course of Eurydice's fate.

With a heavy heart, Zara commanded the ancient weapon to unleash its formidable power. The resonating energy surged across the battlefield, temporarily incapacitating the Empire forces. However, the ancient relic, driven by an unforeseen force, took the intervention a step further. The molecular structure of the once ruthless invaders underwent a profound transformation, disintegrating their bodies into cosmic dust.

As the echoes of conflict subsided, Eurydice's surface bore witness to a momentary stillness. The redirected armada sailed away, and where the Empire forces once stood, only remnants of cosmic dissolution remained. With the ancient weapon at her side, Zara stood amidst the aftermath of her fateful decision.

The fate of Eurydice, which had teetered on the delicate balance between destruction and salvation, was now safe once again from the Terran Empire, if only for the moment.

An Ominous Warning

The UIA command center buzzed with a renewed sense of purpose as the echoes of the cosmic conflict subsided. Orders were issued to dispatch aid to Eurydice, initiating the monumental task of rebuilding the ravaged planet. Teams of engineers and relief personnel were mobilized, guided by a shared commitment to restore Eurydice to its former glory.

In a ceremonial gesture, the UIA gathered to honor the heroes of the Great War. Zara, now a symbol of leadership and resilience, stood at the forefront of the ceremony. The weight of responsibility rested upon her shoulders as she received accolades for her unwavering commitment and strategic brilliance. Promotions were announced, and Zara's rank ascended to new heights, cementing her legacy within the annals of the UIA.

Amidst the celebratory atmosphere, as medals were bestowed and speeches extolled the triumph of unity over adversity, a disembodied voice interrupted the proceedings. Thalia's haunting voice echoed through the chamber, a spectral reminder that the battle was far from over. "Zara," the voice reverberated, "you may have won this battle, but the cosmos is vast, and shadows linger in places unseen. The storm may have abated, but the tempest awaits its moment. Beware, for the echoes of destiny are fickle, and the next chapter of your odyssey is already written in the cosmic winds."

The warning hung in the air, casting a shadow over the ceremony and leaving a palpable sense of foreboding. Now honored and promoted, Zara felt a chill run down her spine as the disembodied voice hinted at challenges yet to come. The battle for Eurydice might have concluded, but the cosmic tapestry had woven a thread of uncertainty into the fabric of her destiny.

The next chapter awaited, and Zara's journey was far from over.